CH00868129

Treasure is Where You Find It

by

Peter Travell

ISBN: 9798460718085

Imprint: Independently published

Cover design by: Art Painter
Library of Congress Control Number: 2018675309
Printed in the United States of America

DEDICATION

*This book is dedicated to the children in my life who have had to listen to
the stories I've told them throughout their childhood whether they liked it or
not!*

Contents

Title Page

Copyright

Dedication

Chapter 1

Chapter 2

Chapter 3

Chapter 4

Chapter 5

Chapter 6

Chapter 7

Chapter 8

Chapter 9

Chapter 10

Chapter 11

Chapter 12

Chapter 13

Chapter 1

It had been raining for three whole days, non-stop, heavy rain! What a time to be on holiday! The three children were becoming very bored, they had played every board and card game the hotel had to offer. The whole idea of going on holiday to this hotel was that it was close to the sea and the whole family had hoped for good weather so that they could spend time on the beach, building sand castles and fishing for crabs and shrimps in the rock pools. A good old-fashioned family holiday is what Dad had called it but now here they were trapped in this old hotel with the rain pouring down outside.

It was a very old hotel set on a low cliff some few hundred yards from the sea. The cliff wasn't sheer but it was very steep and paths wound down from the top to the sandy beach below. It was on the western edge of a wide bay which curved around in a great crescent with the local town set squarely in the middle. Dad had found the hotel advertised in one of those holiday magazines where it had promised 'Good food, rest and relaxation with a wonderful beach for the children to play on while Mum and Dad are able to take it easy'. Well, it might be all of that if it *ever* stopped raining.

The centre of the hotel consisted of the original building, dating back some few hundred years, while several extensions had been added so that it all looked quite modern until you got inside and could see all the old oak beams in the bar and reception areas.

The hotel was run by a very nice lady, Mrs Franklyn, who had bought the hotel some ten or twelve years before with her husband. They had viewed it as a sort of semi-retirement thing to do but, unfortunately, just a few years after they had moved there Mrs Franklyn's husband had died quite suddenly following a heart attack. Mrs Franklyn had then had to run the hotel by herself, a lonely sort of job with very few friends, not many staff but absolutely loads and loads of customers and she was always glad to keep herself busy. She had befriended the children as soon as they had arrived. Mrs Franklyn loved children but had never had any of her own; fate and circumstance had somehow deprived her of that pleasure. Now she enjoyed the company of children all year round by running the hotel, as a 'Real Family Hotel' and she doubted that she would ever give it up. She was a kindly looking lady with a plump bosom and grey hair, that she always wore drawn up into a bun. Sam, the only boy of the family, had remarked when they first arrived at the hotel, that she looked very similar to one of the fairies in Disney's Sleeping Beauty.

"I wonder if she has a magic wand somewhere", Josey had said immediately.

Josey was the youngest of the three children at 9 years of age, while Sam was 10 and Kitty 11. They all had fair hair and fair complexions with bright blue eyes although Josey's eyes in particular could sometimes turn a shade of dark green that glinted wickedly or shone with soft, dewy light when she was sad. Fortunately, she wasn't sad often. Josey was one of life's happier creatures always ready with a smile and a cheery laugh. She had that wonderful gift of being able to make friends with people without apparently trying and without any conscious understanding of what she was doing. So it was that Josey had befriended Mrs Franklyn and chatted to her non-stop whenever their paths crossed. Mrs Franklyn of course was very pleased and made every effort to keep Josey amused while the children were stuck indoors during the bad weather.

On this particular afternoon Mrs Franklyn came across the three children in the hotel lounge playing snakes and ladders for the umpteenth time, terribly bored and feeling quite cross with each other.

"Hello children how are you? Are you enjoying yourselves?" she enquired.

"No, we're not. It's very boring being stuck indoors because of the rain. When is it ever going to end?" Kitty said. Kitty, being 11 years old had developed the attitude she thought was relevant to her station in life as, in her view, she was very nearly a teenager and that meant very nearly grown up!

The three children enjoyed each other's company in the main. They quarrelled occasionally, like all brothers and sisters do but as they had such different personalities, it was easy for them to get along. Kitty was the most level headed when she forgot that she thought she was a teenager. Sam was absolutely totally engaged in the abstract world of adventure stories. He was very clever, strikingly good looking and could be wonderful company whenever he could be prised from his computer game and convinced that he should once again take his place in the real world.

"Oh yes, I wish we could go and play on the beach but Mum says we're not to", said Sam.

"Well she's right", Josey ventured, "If we went to the beach we'd get cold and wet and probably end up with chill".

"Never mind", Mrs Franklyn said soothingly "I saw the weather forecast on TV this morning and they say that by the weekend the weather will clear and we'll have some sunshine".

"That's great but what are we to do 'til then? We've played every game we brought with us and all the games you have in the hotel and now we're really bored", complained Sam who had not been allowed to bring his computer games on this 'Family Holiday'. He'd tried, of course, to slip the computer game into his jacket pocket before they had left the house but Dad had been wise to that move and had retrieved it just as Sam had climbed into the car thinking that he'd been clever enough to get away with it.

"Oh dear Sam", his Dad had said as he reached into the car and retrieved the game from Sam's pocket. "It looks as though you forgot to leave this game behind", and with that he had placed the machine in the front porch, slammed the door and, double locked it behind him. "You won't need that on this holiday. We're going to have fun!" he'd had to say that very loudly to drown the sound of Sam's disgruntled complaints and threats of being very, very bored with "Just the girls to play with!"

Since they'd arrived at the hotel to find the rain had decided it was time for yet another great flood, Sam had wandered the corridors complaining loudly, that "Noah was on his way" and "Should he start building the Ark yet?"

Dad having finally had enough had cornered him one day and told him in no uncertain terms to "Knock it off" and "Go play with your sisters. Next time I'll let you bring the rotten thing if it'll stop you moaning".

To say that Sam was unhappy was an understatement, he was like a junkie without his drug. Dad privately thought that this enforced absence would do his son a lot of good, if only it would stop raining and they could get outside and do something!

Mrs Franklyn understood all this and didn't get upset with the children for the way they had responded. She was a good woman and remembered the frustration of inaction felt by children of their age.

"It is such a shame!" Mrs Franklyn sympathised. "I know, why don't I give you the key to the old attic upstairs? No one has been in there for many years, I remember that it's full of old stuff from before my husband and I moved here. We were always going to clear it out and get rid of the rubbish but somehow we never quite got around to it. You might find some different games up there or perhaps some dressing up clothes to play with. Wait here while I get the key then I'll show you where the attic is and you can play there to your hearts content".

The children all thanked her very much and became quite excited when after two or three minutes Mrs Franklyn re-appeared clutching a very large old-fashioned key in her hand and beckoned them to follow her up the middle staircase of the hotel. This staircase was in the very centre of the hotel, in the very oldest part. It was made of oak beams and planks that made the stair treads. Mrs Franklyn had said that it dated from sometime in the 16th century and that some of the beams in the hotel were from old sailing ships that had been wrecked on the coast nearby.

One night after dinner she had brought in an old man who lived in the town and as entertainment he had sat and told the children, and some of the adults who were also staying at the hotel, stories of what he called the old days of pirates and smugglers, shipwrecks and treasures long since gone and turned to dust.

The old man had been a good storyteller and it had fired the children's imaginations to think that buccaneers and smugglers had used this very hotel in the days gone by. The old man had shown them where, on some of the oak beams there were holes and bits cut out that he said were where they had been used in the galleons and merchantmen when the ships of the sea were the equivalent of today's planes and trains. Sam had immediately asked his Dad to buy him a toy cutlass and an eye patch from one of the local shops and for a short while had terrorised the girls by chasing them up and down the hotel threatening to make them walk the plank or keelhaul them, whatever that meant. Then one swish of the sword too many had brought the wrath of the world upon him.

"Give me that sword at once", Mum had shouted.

"It's not a sword it's a cutlass", Sam had remonstrated but that had only made things worse.

"Give that to me now before you take someone's eye out", and that had been that. Sam's sword had been relegated to the bottom of Mum's suitcase ever since.

He had sulked for a while and walked around mumbling, "It's so unfair". A phrase he'd picked up from his older sister Kitty, but it did no good. Mum was not persuaded to give it back even when he said that he'd be extra, extra careful in future and he was absolutely sure that the bruise on Josey's leg would soon disappear.

"Now you mind that the ghost doesn't get you while you're up here", Mrs Franklyn teased as she led them along the upper corridor.

"Ghost, what ghost?" the children chorused.

The children surrounded Mrs Franklyn and simply would not let her walk another step until she had laughingly explained her remark. "Oh it's nothing my dears", she said, flapping her hands in an attempt to keep the children still and make them calm down. "Legend has it that there's a ghost that walks this old part of the building, some of the people that have stayed here in the past have said they felt some sort of presence. Once I had a psychic investigator to stay, he set up all sorts of equipment in order to capture the ghost on film but nothing ever happened and after a few days, he went away. Quite disappointed he was poor man. I've never seen or heard anything myself but old Martha, who works in the kitchen, swears that she has and won't come near this part of the hotel not for love nor money. You'll have to ask her about it when you see her, she's worked here since before my time and knows quite a lot about the history of this place. You know it's a very old building and this part of the hotel in the very centre dates from the time that it was first built back in the Elizabethan age, when this town was a great harbour and ships from all over the world docked here. Many sailors, gentlemen, ruffians and villains spent their time and money in taverns just like this hotel would have been in those days. As old John told you the other night, some of these old oak beams were taken from the great sailing ships of those days. If you look carefully, you can see old joints and marks in the wood where ropes were pulled across them. It was the practice in those days for people to use old ships timbers as the main support in their houses. I suppose they may have thought it brought good luck or maybe they used them simply because they were available. I don't know. Still that's enough chatter for the moment I must get on I've got lots to do, I really don't think there's anything to worry about". She had realised that Josey had started to look nervously over her shoulder and had pressed herself between the other two children to ensure her back wasn't exposed to any ghost whether it was real or not.

Mrs Franklyn gave a little giggle, ruffled Josey's hair and invited them to follow her once again as she made her way up to the third floor. She led them along the corridor to the end where, set in the middle of the wall, up two steps, was a very old door. "This is the door to the attic", Mrs Franklyn said pointing to what was really quite a small door. "I hope we can get the key to turn in the lock. It has been quite a few years since any one has used it, it might have rusted up".

Mrs Franklyn placed the key in the very large lock and turned. To her surprise, the key turned quite easily and the door swung open with a creak and a groan. She stepped through the doorway with the children crowding behind her and found herself faced with yet another staircase that had perhaps eight or so steps. She fumbled for a light switch and found it just inside the doorway high up on the right hand wall. A single bulb threw a weak light on the stairwell, which would take them up above room height into the roof space.

Mrs Franklyn, who by now was puffing for breath having climbed so many stairs, handed the key to Kitty saying, "Here you are my dear, look after this. You can come and go as you please and you can play with anything you find here. I don't feel like going up there myself. Those stairs look far too steep for my old bones and I'm feeling a little tired today, apart from that it's bound to be terribly dusty and full of spiders".

At the mention of the word spiders Josey leapt back saying "Spiders! Where? Where?" Josey was not terribly fond of spiders and tried to avoid being in the same room as one.

"Spiders won't hurt you!" said Kitty "Come on let's go up and explore!"

The children thanked Mrs Franklyn and promised to look after the key and not make too much noise, and then as Mrs Franklyn stepped back onto the landing they scampered up the stairway and had their first look at the attic. It was enormous; it took up all of the roof space between the bedroom ceilings and the roof tiles. In some places in the corners of the roof, they could see light shining in from outside where the roofing felt had fallen away.

Chapter 2

"Hey! It's a bit dark in here", said Sam "Did either of you bring a torch?"

Of course, neither of the girls had.

"Of course we haven't", said Josey, "Neither have you. We didn't know we would need one did we?"

"Why don't we see if there is another light up here? If there's one for the stairwell there might be one for the attic proper", reasoned Kitty.

The children looked around at the top of the stairs and found a switch fixed to the roof beams at head height just above the top of the stairs. They switched it on and found that it turned on two further lights one at each end of the attic room. They weren't very bright but it was just enough to see by and what they saw was piles and piles of old bric-a-brac. Old dolls prams, gramophones, wardrobes, an old sewing machine, two old armchairs and a sofa and boxes and boxes of goodness knows what.

"Well, let's have a look and see what we can find", said Kitty. They all began to pick their way through the old piles of stuff peering under blankets and lifting boxes, opening doors and drawers hoping to find something interesting, something to play with or perhaps even a treasure!

Of course, everything was covered in dust as Mrs Franklyn had warned them. No one had been in the attic for years and years. Sam, with his usual enthusiasm had immediately started to search the nearest pile of junk and had been rewarded with a face full of dust from an old blanket he'd picked up from the top of a pile of books. He sneezed and coughed until his eyes watered while Kitty and Josey stood there laughing at him. When finally he could see and breathe again Kitty laughingly told him to look at himself in the big mirror propped up against a dresser just behind him. "You look like you could be the ghost Sam. You're so covered in dust you're white as a sheet!"

Sam couldn't help but laugh as he turned and saw himself in the mirror. He did indeed look just like a ghost his hair was grey as was his face and clothes. He turned and made shrieking, ghoulish noises and rushed towards the girls banging his arms across his chest dislodging all the dust and covering them from head to foot.

"Stop it! Stop it! Sam!" Josey yelled trying to cover her face with her hands while Sam yelled even louder and ran up and down sending up clouds and clouds of thick grey dust that swam and sparkled in the sunlight shining through the gaps in the felting. Sam stopped and looked at it in fascination. The dust swirled and twirled in the sunlight, momentarily, seeming to solidify in the form of an outstretched arm before falling in a gentle cloud to the bare floorboards.

"I think that perhaps we should be a little more careful moving this stuff around or we're all going to get into trouble when Mum and Dad see us. Hold still Sam while I try to brush some of the dust off your clothes". In the absence of an adult Kitty took on her customary role of sensible mother figure instead of sulky teenager.

"Did you see the dust?" Sam asked them both while Kitty and Josey tried to brush the worst of the dust from his and their own clothes.

"Yes of course we did", Kitty replied. "We could hardly help it with you shaking it all over us".

"No, no, I don't mean that", Sam said urgently. "I mean the arm, did you see the arm?"

Kitty and Josey looked at each other blankly. "What arm?" they said in unison.

"The dust it formed itself into a sort of arm", Sam insisted "And then it just fell to the floor. It was pointing. Honestly it was I'm not making it up".

"Well I didn't see it", Kitty said with some firmness.

"Nor did I", Josey affirmed but with a little trepidation. She looked over her shoulder, "Which way was it pointing?" she said with a shiver. Suddenly, she felt it had got quite cold up there in the attic and the talk of ghosts and arms made out of dust wasn't quite what she'd had in mind as an afternoon's entertainment.

"There's nothing here", Kitty scoffed and she punched Sam lightly on the shoulder "He's just trying to scare you Josey take no notice".

Sam thought about protesting but stopped himself and simply shrugged and turned back to the piles of junk behind him. If he insisted then Josey would probably get upset and they'd have to go down and he was now convinced that he would find something really interesting amongst this old jumble. After all, arms and hands didn't make themselves appear for no good reason. There was a good story and an adventure here he was certain of it and this time it wasn't a computer game it was real and he intended that in this game he was to be a real life hero!

They all three started to delve carefully in amongst the bric-a-brac trying very hard not to set up any more dust clouds. Josey found an old dolls house covered in a blanket, it was full of little furniture and had some very tiny dolls all dressed in old style clothes. The gentlemen were in top hats and the ladies in long gowns. There were even some doll servants dressed in frilly caps and black dresses and right at the back, she found a tiny little pram with a baby inside it.

"Come and look at this Kitty", she exclaimed with delight but Kitty by this time was fully involved in uncovering a box of toys and books through which she was rummaging as fast as she could. An old spinning top, a hoop, one of those cup things with a ball attached to it via a piece of string, some packs of old playing cards with some very strange symbols on them and a board of some kind with the alphabet engraved around its edge. She picked the box up and took it to the head of the stairs.

"I think if we find anything we want to play with we should bring it over here near the stairs to make it easier to take down. We might have to get Dad to help us because some of these things are quite heavy", she ventured. "I've found some games and Josey's found a doll's house, what've you found Sam?" Kitty had noticed that Sam was on his hands and knees with his head under an old blanket. His bottom was just about the only thing that was visible and it was wiggling backwards and forwards as if he was having a tug of war with a giant.

"Oh nothing much yet", came Sam's muffled voice.

Kitty lost interest and turned away becoming distracted by another box full of books, which she started to leaf through.

Josey looked around her at Kitty and Sam and saw just how many cobwebs there were in the attic. She determined that she had all she wanted in the dolls' house she could play with that for the rest of the day quite happily. She started to drag the house and its contents over to the head of the stairs when suddenly Sam came flying out backwards from under the blanket and a great big leather and brass bound trunk followed him very quickly. Whatever obstacle there was that had prevented Sam from retrieving the old trunk had suddenly given way and Sam had fallen over backwards dragging the trunk with him.

"Oh Sam do be careful", Josey implored. "You don't want to hurt yourself and don't get yourself any more dirty than you already are."

Sam ignored her totally and bent to the task of unlocking the heavy trunk. It was heavy; it was big, brown leather with a great big lid. Each side was bound with brass and it had great brass hinges and a heavy lock in the centre. He couldn't understand why the trunk hadn't moved when he first pulled it, as there was nothing wedging it in. When it finally moved, it was almost as if someone had let it go, as if there had been someone holding onto the other end. He'd even looked behind the trunk to make sure that Kitty or Josey hadn't been playing a trick on him but there was nothing there, very strange. However, he dismissed it from his mind believing that there must have been a nail or something in the old floor on which the trunk had snagged. Now what he had to do was get the lock open but without a key how was he to do that? He tried to prise up the hasp that held the lid to the body of the trunk but it wouldn't move. He searched around the floor under the blanket looking for a key. No such luck. He sat down on the floor and tried to reason it out. If someone had put this trunk up here then it stood to reason that they would also have put the key somewhere but if the trunk contained treasure then of course they wouldn't have been stupid enough to leave the trunk unlocked or with the key in it. No, it would be hidden somewhere in the attic and he had to find it.

This was just like one of his computer games; find the key to undo the trunk and get the weapon or the treasure that was hidden inside. For some reason Sam immediately thought of the arm that he saw when it solidified from the dust. Now where had it been pointing? In his computer games, there was always a clue like that. If he remembered correctly, it had pointed back over to the stairs. He sat on the floor and looked past Josey and Kitty who were struggling to move their finds across the attic to the stair top. He looked past them at the wall and at the ceiling. The light from the two bulbs was very weak and threw shadows across the end wall and the stairs. However, there was one shadow deeper than the others were. Was that a sort of recess in the wall at the side of the stairs, where the roof started to slope towards the eaves? He couldn't be sure. He clambered up and stepped over the junk that Kitty and Josey had moved out of the way to get to their treasures, he dropped to his knees and crawled along the wall to the left of the stairs aiming for the darkest point.

"Sam what are you doing? You're going to get filthy." Josey almost screamed at him. More because he had kicked over some of her dolls in his scramble than any real concern that she felt for his well-being.

Sam ignored her shout and stretched forward as far as he could, groping with the fingers of his right hand into the shadow and hollow that he'd found. A great hairy spider suddenly sprinted down his arm causing him to shriek and shake his arm wildly in the air trying to dislodge the thing before it reached his shoulder. Unfortunately, when the brute did finally let go it was at the point in the trajectory that took it flying through the air to land directly on Josey's head! She screamed and shook her head running her hands through her hair desperate to be rid of the awful creature. Kitty came to the rescue and very bravely snatched the thing from Josey's back setting it down in a corner to see it scuttle gratefully away.

Josey threatened Sam with terrible and dire retaliation "I'll get you Sam. You did that on purpose!" she shouted.

"I didn't honestly Josey. Really I didn't I just shook my arm to get rid of it and it sort of landed on you", he added lamely. "Anyway there's something here in this little alcove and I think it might be the key to that old trunk I've been trying to open. Just stop shouting for a moment and let me get it and I'll let you look in the trunk with me".

"Don't want to look in the rotten old trunk", she replied. "I want to get my dolls' house downstairs and away from these spiders. There might be rats as well", she added as an afterthought. "Come on let's go quickly".

Sam ignored her again and once more groped in the hole and this time his fingers touched on something solid. Triumphantly he withdrew his hand holding a key. Either he was very lucky or the dust arm he had seen really had pointed him in the right direction. Convinced more than ever that this must some clever game devised especially to keep him amused Sam made his way as quickly as possible back to the trunk. The two girls having seen the key and sensing his excitement joined him and watched while he inserted the key into the lock and turned. Reluctantly the lock yielded to the pressure and the key turned completely. Sam grasped the edge of the lid and heaved upwards. Once again, a billow of dust flew into the air and turned Sam into a look alike of the 'Ghost of Christmas Past'. Sam couldn't have cared less. Suppressing an almost overwhelming desire to cough up the entire contents of his chest cavity Sam eagerly delved inside the trunk.

Kitty and Josey couldn't help themselves; they crowded round while Sam unpacked the items that were jumbled inside. He snatched up a pirate's hat and a cutlass that were lying on top of the pile. Whooping and yelling he jumped up and swished and stabbed at the air while the girls took the opportunity to see what other treasures the old chest contained. Josey got there first and found an old spyglass or telescope, which she thought was just amazing. It was brass and very dusty and dirty but when she rubbed the dust from both ends and opened the telescope to its full length she found that it actually worked and holding it up to her eye she could see the detail of the roof where the light was streaming in.

"I bet we'll be able to see right out to sea with this", she cried. "Oh how exciting. Let's take it down stairs now so we can look out of the window with it".

"Not yet", said Kitty. She was trying to avoid being hit by Sam, who was madly rushing up and down brandishing the cutlass in one hand and waving the pirate's hat in the other. As well as Josey who was standing in the middle of the attic twirling around eagerly trying to see into every nook and cranny with the spyglass, which was so large that she could barely hold it up to her eye for more than 30 seconds at a time.

Kitty knelt down in front of the chest and started to take out the remaining items. The first thing she came across was a square of folded cloth. It was black with bits of white on it. She stood up and started to unfold it, catching the other's attention they came over and helped. It was an enormous flag, a 'Jolly Roger' showing the skull and crossbones, white on black. It wasn't in very good condition having several holes and tears.

"Oh look", cried Sam "I bet those holes were made by bullets and things, I wonder who this all belonged to? It seems quite real doesn't it?"

Somehow seeing the 'Jolly Roger' sobered them all as they thought about where this might have come from and what use had been made of it in the past.

A real pirate's sea chest with a real cutlass, hat and telescope! At any minute, they felt as if something awful might jump up out of the chest and engulf them all in a blood-curdling scream.

Draping the 'Jolly Roger' over a nearby armchair Sam went back to the sea chest and peered inside. An old glove with two fingers missing was next out.

"Hey look at this I wonder if his hand was in it when the fingers got lost?" Sam said with sort of ghoulish relish placing his hand inside and wiggling it under Josey's nose. Josey covered her face in her hands and whimpered a bit. Kitty gave Sam a sharp push to make him stop his teasing.

"Oh you're no fun Josey", said Sam as he dropped the glove back in the sea chest. He scrabbled around at the bottom and brought out a big black bible covered in dust, which he immediately dropped to the floor because underneath it was what looked like a sort of wallet. It was made of some sort of material covered in wax or something; it was smooth and slightly sticky. Sam pulled it out and as the girls gathered round, he slowly untied the string that held it together.

Sam unfolded the wallet and found that it had quite a few layers and pockets. He gently probed into each of the pockets in turn with his fingers. Carefully, because it didn't feel very nice.

"Whatever this wallet is made of I don't know but it feels horrible, all sort of slick and slimy", Sam said in a shaky voice. He was feeling very nervous for some reason, all the fun, laughter and raucous behaviour of a minute or two ago had suddenly left him and he felt as if he were doing something forbidden. As his fingers slid into the biggest pocket at the very back of the wallet and he touched what felt like paper. His mind suddenly threw up the picture of the hand made from dust, which he had seen swirling in the air just before he found the chest. It made him shiver and hesitate.

Kitty said impatiently "Come on Sam, what's in there, have you found something?"

"A piece of paper I think but I just felt a bit cold, I'm not sure I want to get it out up here. I think I feel a bit scared. You don't think that the hand I saw was the ghost of the pirate who owned this chest do you?"

Both Kitty and Josey looked at him in amazement; he had gone as white as a ghost under the layer of dust that still clung to his face.

Josey looked over her shoulder into the darkest recesses of the attic and said in a quavering voice, "I don't like this Kitty. Let's take it downstairs where it's light. Let's look at it there. If there are ghosts they won't come if it's light will they?"

Kitty scoffed and gave a little laugh trying to be very brave and very grown up "There's no such thing as ghosts, don't be silly both of you. But if you want to go down at least we'll be able to see it properly."

In truth, Kitty had felt a shiver run down her spine and she was feeling as if all she wanted to do was run away as fast her legs would carry her but she fought down the feeling of panic, which gripped her and as calmly as she could said, "Come on then let's go. We'll leave all the other stuff and come back for it later."

Quickly the children jumped to their feet and scrambled for the door pushing and jostling each other in their haste to get out of the attic and down the stairs as quickly as they could.

They all felt as if something or somebody was behind them. Not one of them turned to look behind them a cold draft had sprung up and raised the hairs on the back of their necks as they pushed their way across the attic and through the piles of junk. As if they had wings on their feet, they flew down the stairs jumping the last few steps onto the landing and quickly slamming the door shut behind them. Breathless Kitty turned the key in the lock shutting the imagined horror behind the door. She led the way down the corridor, saying, "Come on you two let's go to Sam's room and examine it properly."

"Did you feel it? What was it?" Josey asked in a small, frightened voice.

"Feel what?" said Kitty thrusting her chin out. "There was nothing there. It just got a bit cold that's all. Now come on let's go."

Sam and Josey looked at each other meaningfully while allowing Kitty to bustle them away as quickly as she could. In truth they had all felt something whether it was a ghost or just their over-heated imaginations they didn't know but Kitty felt that as the eldest she must act like a grown up and in her opinion that's what a grown up would do. She had noticed that very often grown ups would simply deny that anything was wrong when it was obvious to everyone that there was. She had learnt to deny what she didn't understand. It seemed to her that was what she was meant to do and she supposed that somehow it made life easier. Certainly, this way she didn't have to think about it or investigate it but inside her head, she knew that she had felt something she had never experienced before.

Sam's room was on the second floor still in the oldest part of the hotel and directly below the attic room door. The children skidded down the stairs, along the corridor and pushed quickly into Sam's room closing the door behind them. They threw themselves on the bed puffing and panting.

"Well I don't care what you say Kitty, I think there was a ghost up there. I felt all the hairs on my neck stand up when we went to go", Josey said in a small but defiant voice.

"Don't be silly Josey. I told you there's no such thing as ghosts. What do you think Sam?" said Kitty turning to him with a 'Don't you be silly too' look.

Sam privately agreed with Josey but felt that as a boy he couldn't afford to appear to be sissy in any way, so he merely grunted and said, "Well I've never seen a ghost but if I do I'll chop them into bits." He then leapt to his feet and swished the cutlass through the air in a threatening manner.

"Don't you worry Josey. If any ghosts come near I'll defend you." He clapped the pirate's hat on his head and struck a very ridiculous pose with his hand on his hip and the cutlass thrust out in front of him. The girls dissolved into laughter and giggles, which only served to make Sam furious. He stamped his feet shouting, "OK you two, if you're going to laugh at me you can get out and when a ghost does come to get you you'll be own your own." He stamped to the door and opened it shouting, "Come on, get out, get out", looking as though he might burst into tears at any moment.

Kitty managed to hold her face together and nudged Josey saying, "Sorry Sam we don't want to go and we do want you to protect us, it's just that you looked so funny standing there waving that sword about. I really think you ought to put it down in case you hurt someone and if Mum or Dad see you with it they'll take it away, so perhaps you should close the door and find a place to hide it before they come along to find out what all the fuss is about."

Sam grudgingly saw the sense in what Kitty had said and reluctantly closed the door, looking around for a place to hide the treasured cutlass. "I'll put it in the wardrobe for the moment and find a better place for it later. I wonder if Mrs Franklyn will let me take it home. Oh, but then I'd have to tell Mum and Dad and they'd never let me keep it. Oh bother why do grown ups have to spoil all the fun?"

"Well if we keep quiet about all this then at least while we're on holiday you can keep it if you promise on your honour to be careful and not use it unless we're in danger. No swishing it around and taking lumps out of people like you normally do. You know how clumsy you are sometimes Sam." Kitty was once again playing her accustomed role of Big Sister. Sam looked back at her with a sulky frown marring his otherwise handsome features.

Josey seeing that a row was about to develop butted in saying, "Oh come on you two. Put the sword down Sam and let's have a look at what's in the wallet. I'm not sure if there was a ghost or not but if there was it had something to do with the contents of that." She pointed at the wallet that was sticking out of Sam's back pocket. This comment brought the other two up sharply, they had been about to descend into another bickering, picky row, which had been known to culminate in a shouting match and sometimes a fight.

"Alright", he said putting the sword in the wardrobe on the floor behind his shoes. "But don't either of you two touch it. It's mine understand."

Closing the wardrobe door, he pulled the wallet out of his pocket and they all sat together on the bed while once again he carefully unfolded it and gently pulled the stiff, heavy piece of paper from the back flap. It was very thick paper; they imagined it was what parchment was like although they had never seen any. It had been folded several times and as Sam unfolded it, he had to be very careful not to tear it.

"Be careful Sam", Kitty had admonished, "It looks as if it'll tear quite easily where the folds have been. I wonder how old it is. It really does look very worn and there are marks on it see there", she said pointing at a sort of curly brown ring that had obviously been made by the parchment getting wet and then drying out.

Sam with a real effort slowed himself down and carefully fold by fold slowly exposed the whole of the paper. It was big, twice the size of an exercise pad. It was yellowish in colour, with water marks all over the paper but as he turned it over, they all gasped.

"It's a map!" Josey exclaimed, "A real pirate's map. There might be treasure."

Chapter 3

Sam's hands started to shake with excitement, so much that Kitty quickly said, "Put it down on the bed Sam so that we can all see properly." Sam dropped the map onto the bed and all three of the children knelt around exclaiming and gasping in wonder and amazement.

The map depicted what appeared to be the outline of a coast shown in brown and the sea roughly marked in blue. At least that's what they supposed it was, as there seemed to be a river running up from South to North. In the top right hand corner of the map a small compass setting had been drawn showing which way was north. The children had learned about the points of the compass in Cubs, Brownies and Scouts and had learnt the basics of following and understanding maps. The map seemed to show a bay much like the one in which the hotel was situated but it looked nothing like the town in which they were staying. It had only a small number of buildings and there weren't any roads shown at all.

"Look", said Kitty pointing at the shapes on the map. "These must be buildings of some sort. Two lots, one group over here on the Western side of the bay and another lot over here in what seems to be the centre of the village. There aren't that many are there? It must be quite a small place perhaps just a little village somewhere. What a pity it doesn't show a place name then we'd know where it was."

"Don't be ridiculous", Sam scoffed. "Whoever heard of a treasure map with place names on it. It's a secret map isn't it, stupid."

"You're so horrible sometimes Sam", said Josey interjecting trying once again to head off a potential fight between the two. "But what's this wiggly line running across here?" she distracted them pointing to a faint line drawn in black that lead from one of the supposed buildings in more or less a straight line towards the sea. The line stopped before it reached the blue of the sea and ended in what looked like a smudge of ink. The smudge was on a line where the map had been folded and so it was very difficult to see whether it was a smudge, an inkblot, a water mark or simply the fold itself.

The children all sat back with their legs folded up underneath them and looked at each other.

"I think it's a real Treasure Map", Sam said. "It makes sense doesn't it? I mean we know that there used to be pirates around here. We found it in an old chest, there's the cutlass, the hat and the spyglass. It all seems real to me and it looks centuries old. I mean to say it wouldn't be here just for a joke would it?" Sam added a little lamely, as the two girls looked at him without uttering a word. Shock was registered on the both their faces as the girls considered Sam's words.

"I think you're right Sam", Josey ventured "But what does it show? There's no 'X' marking the spot, there's nothing here that says that it is a Treasure Map but it must be, why draw a map like this if it isn't showing something of interest?"

"Mmmmm!" Kitty considered. "Well what shall we do with it? I suppose the right thing to do would be to show Mum and Dad or give it to Mrs Franklyn after all we did find it in her trunk, in her attic."

"Oh No!" said Sam and Josey together.

"No, no." Sam almost shouted. "Mrs Franklyn said we could play with whatever we found up there. Well, we'll just play with it some more before we give it back and we don't want to tell Mum and Dad because they'll take it away or tell us not to be so silly. If we do that we'll never get to discover whether it really is a Treasure Map or not."

"OK. Let's agree that we're going to try to discover what it really is before we do anything else", said Kitty with enthusiasm. "But we all have to keep this secret. Don't go blabbing Josey when you get upset about something, you know you do that sometimes."

"No I don't", said Josey in mock shock. She did sometimes and she knew it. Occasionally, when one of the others had upset her and she needed a bit of a cuddle she would climb on to Dad's lap and talk to him about whatever Kitty and Sam were up to and he'd give her a squeeze and make her feel better.

"OK but let's agree this time that we don't talk to anyone about this not even Dad, not until we know what it is properly. Alright?" Kitty put her hand forward into the air over the map and the other two placed their hands on top of hers.

"Agreed!" they all chorused moving their hands up and down in one movement.

"Now let's see if we can work out what this is and where it is." Kitty led the discussion.

"Well, that's got to be the sea", said Sam pointing at the blue bit.

"And that's the coast line", chimed in Josey pointing at the brown line that ran in a sort of curved wiggle from the top to bottom of the page.

"This must be a river and these are buildings of some sort", said Kitty.

"It's a bay. See here there are headlands jutting out at the top and the bottom of the map. Hang on we're in a bay here aren't we?" said Sam jumping up and moving to the window for a look.

Sam's room faced the sea while the girls' bedroom, which they shared, was on the other wall of the hotel and looked over part of the town. Kitty and Josey joined Sam at the window and they saw that indeed there were in a bay with headlands to the right and left of them.

"That's a bit of a coincidence isn't it?" Kitty mused, "Still I suppose there must be oodles of seaside towns that are in bays but it might just be that this is an old map of this area. Trouble is I don't know how we're going to find out. Nothing on here looks like what we've seen of the town. I mean the town's really quite big compared to these few buildings shown on here", she said pointing to the cluster of buildings shown on the map.

"Wonder if there's anything else in here?" said Sam carefully sliding his fingers into another flap in the wallet. "Nothing here. Oh wait here's something", he cried.

"What, what!" chorused the girls impatiently.

"Hold on a moment, here it is." Sam gently drew out yet another piece of paper this one was quite small but just as old, folded and creased. Gently opening out the small piece of paper Sam was astonished to see some really old fashioned, sloping writing running from top to bottom of the paper. Faded in places and difficult to decipher he started to read.

Billy Bones will have his say
That Treasure is where ye find it
Where dead men's eyes stare up and pray
Beneath the rocks ye'll find it

Now ye've got the treasure map
T'is in ye'r hands this day
There may be more than one mishap
Afore you end the play

The tunnel's hidden. Ye must take care
My treasure it be waiting
Down in the depths, beware, beware
Straight down below with Satan

Look to the window up on high
Ye see the gleaming gold
It's there ye see, tho' times gone by
Ye have to, must be bold

Now I will come and spike your gun
I must be here it seems
Until the treasure it be gone
To feed some poor man's dreams

For this I tell ye mortal fool
I hid it good, and well
The bones of my old faithful crew
Still guard it now, farewell

"Oh my goodness", Josey cried. "He's going to come. His ghost is going to come! That must have been who was in the attic. I don't like this Sam! I don't like this Kitty! Let's put the map back in the trunk. Let's forget we ever saw it. I don't want to see a ghost".

Sam and Kitty looked at Josey who was by now near to tears. In truth, they both felt a little shaken themselves but suddenly Sam said, "I'm not afraid of some old ghost and at least it proves that the map is genuine and not just some silly old piece of paper. Pity it goes on about him coming to see us but if I keep the map in here with me tonight then his ghost will come in here, if it comes anywhere and I'll be ready for him don't you worry."

This was a very brave little speech from Sam and the girls both looked at him in amazement.

"Well Sam that's very brave", Kitty finally gasped as Sam once again struck a fierce pose trying very hard to look mean and tough but managing only to look a little scared. "But I'm really sure there's no such thing as a ghost and I'm pretty sure that after all this time Cap'n Billy is not going to be visiting anybody. I don't think there's anything very much to worry about. If you like perhaps we could all sleep together tonight. You can sneak into our room once everyone's in bed and asleep. There's more space in our room and you can bring your duvet. We'll push the beds together and sleep until the sun comes up."

"Oh yes that's a good idea", said Josey much comforted. She hadn't liked the thought of Sam being by himself and all being together gave her more courage than she would have felt left by herself or with just Kitty for company. She made up her mind that she would occupy the middle space with the other two one on either side.

"Now, let's have a look at that map again. The rhyme said something about beneath the rocks. I must say I didn't like the bit about 'Dead men's eyes' that sounded a bit spooky what do you think he meant by that?" Kitty asked with a little shiver.

"I reckon that he's talking about the men he killed after they had buried his treasure" Sam replied. "That's what all the pirates I've ever read about did. They got men to carry the treasure to some secret place and bury it on the promise of having a share in it when they came back to dig it up. The chief pirate would want to keep the treasure all to himself and would kill them all and bury them in the hole with the treasure. To guard it 'til the end of the world or the Cap'n came back for it." This last phrase Sam said in a sort of Long John Silver voice, all hoarse whisper and with a cackling laugh at the end.

"Oh just shut up Sam", Josey cried, "I don't even want to think about it. I bet there's no treasure really and certainly not any dead men guarding some rotten hole in the ground. If there were treasure, why wouldn't it have been found and dug up by now? You read about treasure hunters all the time. People just wandering around with metal detectors and stuff. It if ever did exist I bet it's gone by now and all the dead men with it." Josey was really quite scared now and she had said this just to try to bolster her flagging courage.

"Oh I don't know Josey", Kitty interjected, "I think it depends quite how well the treasure was hidden. Usually pirates' treasure was buried out on the Spanish Main, wherever that is, where they did all their pirating. I don't think many pirates would have brought the treasure back to England and then buried it. Treasure hunters wouldn't necessarily be looking around a small town in this country, if that's where the treasure is and we don't know that yet but I think there's a good chance that it might still be there, wherever there is and that's what we've got to do; find out where is this place that's on the map." Kitty pulled the map towards her and looked at it very closely, in particular at the little wiggly line that ran from one of the buildings down towards the sea, ending in the small smudge.

"This building is set apart from the others and this little line starts from inside the building as far as I can see. Whoever drew this tried to show a bit of detail in the house 'cos it seems like they've drawn in some walls. Oh bother, it's so difficult to see properly. What we need is a magnifying glass. I wonder if there's one anywhere in the hotel? Josey, why don't you go and find Mrs Franklyn and ask? She likes you best and if she has one, I'm sure she'll lend it to you. Don't tell her why you really want it just say that you want it to study the little dolls you found in that dolls house in the attic."

"OK. I'll see if I can find her, but what are you two going to be doing while I'm gone?" Josey enquired.

"Well, what we've got to do is to find out what place this map is really depicting." Kitty said thoughtfully.

"Depicting. What's that mean?" Sam scoffed, "Stop using such big words Kitty you're only a kid stop acting so grown up. You're not our Mum so why don't you stop telling us what to do all the time. No one put you in charge and it's my map I found it so if anyone's going to be in charge it should be me."

"Depicting means – well it means depicting", Kitty stumbled over the explanation "Showing, representing, where it really is, stupid."

"Don't you call me stupid! You're the one who's stupid!" Sam roared jumping to his feet and going purple in the face.

"Stop it, stop it!" Josey cried. "If you two go on like this we'll never get anywhere. Why can't we work together? No one has to be in charge do they? Let's just all give our ideas on what we should do next and how we can find out where this place is supposed to be, where the map is 'depicting'", Josey struggled with the word "and then we'll decide what's best".

"All right", Kitty grumbled, "But before we do anything else I think we ought to hide the map just in case Mum or Dad or Mrs Franklyn walk in and find it. Where shall we hide it?"

"Well it's got to be somewhere in here. In my room", Sam was still miffed. "I need to be able to defend it and I'm the one with the cutlass".

"Ok Sam", Kitty replied with a resigned sort of shrug, "Where are you going to put it? It's got to be somewhere really safe where no one will look when they're making the bed or cleaning the room or where Mum might see it when she's putting your clothes away."

The children scoured the room, discussed and rejected several ideas such as behind the curtain, under the pillow, under the bed, back of the wardrobe, in Sam's dressing gown that was hanging on the back of the bedroom door. Until suddenly Sam exclaimed, "I know. I've got it. We'll put it under the wardrobe".

The wardrobe was quite old and made of pine. It had one of those curly sorts of bottoms on the front that was cut into a small pattern and which, if your fingers were small enough you could reach under. Sam quickly took the wallet and pushed it under the wardrobe just far enough so that it was out of sight but close enough that he could just reach it with the tips of his fingers and pull it out again. He practised putting it in and taking it out several times to make sure while the girls walked about the room looking at the bottom of the wardrobe to ensure that it could not be seen from any angle. Just as they had finished hiding the very precious map, Mum came bursting into the room.

"I've been all over the hotel looking for you three", she stormed, "It's dinner time. Didn't you hear the dinner gong? Now come along all three of you go and wash your hands and get yourselves down to the dining room as quickly as you can. And no backchat please!" she added as she saw

Sam about to protest that they'd been in his room all the time.

The children weren't the only ones who were fed up with staying indoors because of the rain. Mum was equally fed up and was taking it out on anyone that didn't do exactly as they were told, even before they were told it! Sam decided not to pursue the injustice. He'd been on the sharp end of Mum's tongue before and it wasn't something that he relished experiencing again. Grumbling gently beneath his breath he and the girls stumped out of the room and ran to the bathroom along the landing where they all quickly flicked water over their hands and faces and rejoined Mum who was waiting, with tapping toe, outside the door.

"Right come on, quickly now, downstairs into the dining room before we miss dinner. Dad's there already and I expect that he'll have ordered for you so no complaints, eat what your given", Mum instructed, still in a terrible mood.

The children hurried downstairs leaving Mum in their wake and made their way to the table Dad was saving for them all.

Chapter 4

"Hiya", said Dad. "Where have you lot been all afternoon?"

"Oh this and that", said Kitty airily.

"We've been up in the attic", Josey joined in excitedly, only to receive a warning nudge from Sam who was in the process of sitting down next to her. "Yes", he exclaimed. "Mrs Franklyn gave us the key to the attic and we've been up there finding stuff to play with."

"There's heaps of junk and stuff up and it's quite dusty", Kitty joined in, "But we've found some toys and things that we'd quite like your help to bring some down" Kitty continued, "Perhaps after dinner you could come up and help us?"

In truth none of the children were very interested in playing with the things from the attic now that they'd found the map. However, Kitty had reasoned, very wisely that if they had toys to play with they could remain out of their parents sight without there being too much fuss and most importantly without their parents wanting to know exactly what they were doing.

"Yes OK, I don't mind", Dad replied, pleased that the children had stopped grumbling about the weather and being so bored.

"Don't mind what", said Mum coming into the dining room and taking her place at the table between Kitty and Sam.

There was always competition between the children as to who would get to sit next to Dad. It was in some ways unfortunate there were three because only two could sit next to him at any one time. It was the same when they went out together only two could hold his hands and so they had some sort of loose rota where they took it in turns. Somehow, Josey always seemed to end up sitting next to him or holding his hand and the others didn't mind so much these days. Most of the time Kitty felt far too grown up to hold Dad's hand anyway and Sam being a boy, simply liked to walk along chatting. Hand holding had been left far behind. However, Josey was still young enough and affectionate enough not to care what the others thought, she wanted to sit with her Dad and she would if she could.

"Oh the children have found some new toys to play with in the attic and they've asked me to help bring them downstairs", Dad replied.

"Oh good. Perhaps that'll keep you all quiet for a few hours", Mum said still grumpy. "But it will have to wait until we've been for a walk after dinner. It's stopped raining so we've decided we'll get out while we can. We've still got a couple of hours of daylight left and it'll be so nice to get some fresh air." Mum's smile softened her face and her mood.

The children all looked up glad that Mum was happy again. "Oh yes let's walk down to the sea-front." Kitty cooed.

"We can skim stones into the waves", Sam said waving his arm wildly in the air practising the art of stone skimming in his mind.

Mum caught the glass Sam nudged with his arm before it spilt all the water while Josey expressed her opinion that, "Looking in the rock pools would be nice."

"I think we'll leave the beach until another time", Dad replied, "Don't want us all to get wet just before bed time do we? Perhaps we can do all that tomorrow, for tonight we'll just have a gentle stroll down into the town and a walk along the front. Once we're back I'll help you get the stuff down from the attic and then it'll be almost time for bed."

The children agreed excitedly and in their new found happiness all thought of Cap'n Billy Bones' dire warning in the rhyme they'd found disappeared from their minds as they looked forward to getting out of the hotel at long last and into the town.

After dinner, Mum sent them all to collect their coats and hand in hand, they strolled into town smiling, laughing and playing as they walked along.

While they were walking into town Kitty cleverly started to talk about the history of the town and the stories the old local had told the previous evening.

"Do you think there really were pirates around here Dad?" she asked

"Well I'm not sure about pirates", Dad replied, "But there certainly were smugglers in this area and that's almost as good as pirates. They made heaps of money smuggling in contraband from abroad and avoiding the Revenue Men. I've been reading a book I found in the Hotel's library, it's all about the history of this area and in particular about one chap who went by the name of Cap'n Billy Bones. He was quite infamous and spent many years smuggling and avoiding being caught by the law. To the people in this area he is something of a legend. Of course, in the end he was caught, he was tried and sentenced to death by the local judiciary. Strange when you think about it because they were just the sort of people, all the local landowners and such like, who bought the smuggled goods from him in the first place. So hypocritical, but he was hanged from the gibbet in the town square. It's not there now, it was demolished a long time ago but the tourist board have put up a plaque commemorating the event. Billy Bones is quite a tourist attraction round here. The book says that according to local legend he went to his death carrying the secret of his hidden treasure with him. Plenty of people have searched for it over the years but apparently, no one has ever found it. Probably it didn't ever exist, just the local people of the time making up stories of his wealth once he was dead and gone. You know how these things are, everything gets exaggerated over the years. Still it's an interesting read if you'd like to borrow it Kitty I'll dig it out for you when we get back to the hotel."

"Oh yes please Dad", Kitty said quickly, "I'd really like to read about Cap'n Billy. Are there any maps and things in it? It'd be interesting to see what the town looked like in his day."

"Oh yes. There are quite a few reproductions of hand drawn maps of the area. Quite interesting really", Dad replied. "And there's a wonderful story in there about Cap'n Billy's ghost, which is said to walk the halls and corridors of the very hotel we're staying in. Do you know that there have been several sightings over the years, not lately though", he added quickly as he saw Josey's face turn toward him with a worried frown. "No. No. The last one was

50 years ago or more but it's interesting none the less. Several people over the years have said they've felt some sort of presence." Dad was warming to the story now, "Apparently it's felt or seen most often in the very old part of the hotel, down by reception and the stairs above. You know the central stairs that lead from reception up to the second floor. The most common sighting has been a disembodied hand and arm, accompanied by a very eerie and deathly chill. No one has heard anything, no voices or murmurings or anything. Just cold and then a vague sort of feeling that they'd seen a hand. No one could categorically swear that it was a hand. They all said they just sort of felt that they'd seen a hand. Very unsatisfactory. Nothing you could actually pin down although I think the people that did see it or think they'd seen it were very probably scared out of their wits. I'm not sure that I could talk with any great certainty if I'd seen a ghost. I'd have been too busy running in the opposite direction."

"Do you think ghosts really exist Dad? Are we going to see Cap'n Billy's ghost?" Josey exclaimed in horror.

"Oh no I don't think so, after all we haven't seen him up until now have we and we've been here quite a few days already. No I think if there were such things as ghosts somebody somewhere would have proved it by now. There have been all sorts of studies of supposed ghosts and they've all turned out to be fake or not exist at all. Didn't Mrs Franklyn say the other day that she'd had a ghost hunter here and he'd not found a thing. Well there you are then. Nothing to worry about Josey. Come on I'll race you to the corner and loser buys the ice-creams." Dad with Josey and Sam on his heels ran swiftly away leaving Kitty to walk along with her Mum.

"What do you think Mum?" Kitty enquired, "Do you think there are such things as ghosts?"

"Well", Mum replied thoughtfully, "I'm really not very sure Kitty. There have been so many reports of people, especially young children seeing ghosts or apparitions of some sort. I suppose it could be overheated imagination or excitement or even wishful thinking, but I do think that probably there is something in it. Something we don't yet understand or that we're too scared to admit to ourselves. One thing I do think is that if there are ghosts they can't do us any harm at all. They may just appear and make us frightened but that's only because we don't have any experience or explanation for them. I really don't think real or not that there's anything to worry about Kitty, but I really do think that your Dad should stop telling you such stories, especially in front of Josey; you know what she's like. We'll have her up all night worrying that a ghost is going to come and get her!" Mum laughed as she said this and took Kitty's arm in hers as they quickly caught up with the others who were already tucking into very large ice cream cornets complete with the obligatory sticks of chocolate. Dad had given his chocolate to Josey, as he didn't much care for that type of confection, far too sweet for him these days. He always complained that it made his teeth ache although he wasn't averse to sharing a big bar of fruit and nut every now and then. In truth, he just wanted to spoil Josey and this was an easy, silly way of showing his affection for her.

"Come on you two slow coaches", he called, "Want an ice-cream?"

Kitty immediately joined in choosing a pistachio flavoured ice cream while Mum declined citing her ongoing 'Battle of the Bulge' while patting her stomach and hips.

As the family moved away from the ice cream shop Mum and Dad fell into step with Mum affectionately taking Dad's arm. The children scampered on ahead running along the road and down on to the rocky beach. As they quickly licked their ice-cream cones and munched on the chocolate, they discussed what they'd learned from their little chat with Dad.

"Well, if this book that Dad found has got maps in it we ought to be able to match them up with our map", Kitty ventured.

"Oh that was so clever of you Kitty", Josey chimed in, "You got all that information out of Dad without letting either him or Mum know what we're up to."

"Yes." said Sam, "You're pretty sneaky Kitty. So what do we do next?"

Sam, who had wolfed his ice-cream long since, started to skim pebbles across the wave tops and the girls gathered round admiring or jeering his more useless efforts.

"When we get back to hotel we've got to get Dad to help us move the stuff down from the attic that will give us cover while we work out the location of our map. We can't do anything else until we know where to look can we?" Kitty whispered quietly. "Once we've found out whether it's this part of this coast or not and which building our map is showing we can decide on our next step." She went on.

"Don't you mean where our map is *depicting*?" Sam said with obvious relish.

"Oh shut up Sam. If you've got any better ideas then let's have them", Kitty retorted reddening in her anger.

"Oh hold on Kitty. I was only teasing." Sam quickly interjected before Kitty could get into full flow. Sam had seen his sister get into one of her rages before at just the slightest thing and it was not a pretty sight. He did his best to 'head her off at the pass' so to speak before she ended up shouting at him and stomping off and sulking for a couple of days. "I was just joking Kitty. You're right of course that's exactly what we've got to do and when we get back we can all help bring the stuff down from the attic to our rooms as quickly as we can so that we have time to look at the book Dad found before Mum sends us off to bed." He added quickly in the hope that by agreeing with Kitty it would mollify her mood.

"Yes", said Josey knowing exactly what Sam was up to, "Come on let's head back to the hotel now. It's half past eight already and if we're not quick Mum will make us wait until the morning and I want to look at the book tonight."

"OK but be careful not to mention our map when we're looking at the book with Dad", Kitty admonished and turning she scrambled up the beach to where Mum and Dad were waiting, with Josey and Sam trudging up after her.

Sam grumbled to Josey, as they walked together, "I don't know what's wrong with Kitty these days. She gets more and more like Mum. Sometimes you just can't say a thing to her. I guess it's because she's getting all grown up or at least she likes to think she is. Oh well, it was clever of her to find out about the book. Come on Jo let's hurry and catch them up we don't want to be left out of anything". With that he flicked Josey's arm and smiled his big warm smile, took her hand and pulled her up the beach to where Mum, Dad and Kitty were waiting.

Dusk was starting to fall now and as the family made their way back up the hill to their hotel Dad stopped and looked up at the sky, it was beautiful. To the west, the setting sun had turned the sky blood red. The clouds above them and in the east were red on one side, white and grey on the other. The clouds formed a strange pattern, which Dad called herringbone, like the backbone and ribs of a fish once you'd eaten all the meat from it.

"Oh how lovely", Mum sighed looking up.

"Mmm!" Dad grunted in appreciation. "It's going to be a lovely day tomorrow. You know the old saying 'Red sky at night, Shepherd's delight'; it's usually quite accurate. We ought to be able to get out to the beach with any luck."

The children looked at each other. If Dad was right and it was a fine day in the morning that meant they'd have no time to pursue their treasure hunt.

"Oh well even if it isn't a nice day tomorrow at least now we've got some new things to play with", Josey said with a big smile on her face. "Come on Dad let's get up to the hotel and you can help us get them down." She moved ahead of them pulling on Dad's hand to make him step out more quickly.

"Whoa, hold on there Josey what's all the rush?" Dad smiled at her efforts. "All your toys will still be there in five minutes time." But, he walked on with her quickening his step to keep pace with hers, while Sam and Kitty ran on ahead and Mum brought up the rear grumbling that, "Would they all please slow down because she simply couldn't keep up with them, at least not going up this steep hill."

At last, they reached the hotel and the children ran in throwing off their coats as they entered the lobby half-dragging Dad to the foot of the central staircase.
"Children!" Mum shouted as she puffed her way in through the big double doors. "Pick up those coats and hang them up this instant or it'll be straight to bed for all of you."

While the children meekly turned around and grudgingly picked their coats from the floor. Dad turned to Mum and said, "Why don't you go into the bar and order us a couple of drinks and have a little relax while I go with the children to fetch all the stuff down from the attic? I'm sure it won't take that long. Go on off you go, we'll only be a minute or two." He gave Mum a peck on the cheek and gently guided her off across the lobby towards the bar, coming back to help the children arrange their coats in some semblance of order on the pegs and coat stand inside the door.

"Come on then you lot let's get this over with so I can have that drink", he said laughing at them and giving them all a little nudge towards the stairs.

"I've got to get the key", Kitty suddenly remembered. "I'll run up and get it from the bedroom and meet you by the attic door", she called over her shoulder as she hurried away up the stairs.

Josey and Sam took Dad's hands and pulled him towards and up the stairs while he pretended to be old and bent then he picked them both up one under each arm and staggered up a couple of steps until he literally buckled under their weight. "Phew! You've both got very heavy all of a sudden", he puffed, "Either that or I've gotten very old and very weak over the past few days."

"Poor old man", they both sang while pulling him up the rest of the stairs towards the second floor landing where the attic door was located. Just as they reached the second floor, Kitty came skidding up behind them. "Here it is", she cried, "I've got the key" and they all walked quickly towards the door.

Josey, suddenly remembering how she felt when they had left the attic in a scare pressed herself against Dad as he took the key and unlocked the door. This time the lock was quite stiff and Dad had a little struggle with it before he prised it open.
"Must have rusted up over the years." Dad reflected but the children looked at each other with a little shiver remembering how easily the key had turned earlier in the day. Reaching inside Dad turned on the light and led the way upstairs exclaiming when he saw all the junk in the attic. "Surely we're not taking all this lot downstairs. It's mostly just junk and all terribly dusty. Your Mum will have a fit!"

"No just this stuff over here, Dad", Sam quickly replied pointing out the dolls house, the sea chest and few other odds and ends, that the children had stacked up earlier that day.

"OK what's in the chest Sam?" Dad asked.

"Nothing very much", Sam replied, "Just some old books and things that I thought I might like to have a look at."

"OK. Then let's put some of this other stuff inside, then you and I can carry it down between us while the girls carry the dolls house." Dad instructed, and they filled the chest and staggered down the stairs closing and locking the attic door.

The children looked at each other in some relief. They had all been a bit scared of going up to the attic after what had happened in the afternoon but with Dad with them, they hadn't felt scared at all. There hadn't seemed to be any threat and certainly, it hadn't seemed as cold up there as it had before. Between them, they carried the stuff down to the first floor and deposited the chest in Sam's room and the dolls house with all its little figures, plus some books, that Kitty had chosen, in the girl's room.

"OK let's leave that stuff and go down to Mum." Dad rounded them up and closed the bedroom door behind them leading the way down.

"Before we go to Mum can we go to the library and find that book you told us about please Dad?" Kitty wheedled.

"OK. OK. Come on then but then you children must leave Mum and me to have a quiet little drink together. You can either sit with us in the bar, go to the TV lounge or stay in the library. Whatever you like only you must be good and not get into any trouble. I don't think Mum would appreciate any aggravation tonight", Dad remonstrated with them.

"Oh Dad. How can you say that? We're always good", Sam said with a bit of a smirk.

"Yes right Sam", Dad pulled a face. "As good as a room full of vipers. Now I mean what I say any trouble and it'll be straight to bed for the lot of you. Understand?" He looked at them threateningly and they all hung their heads and nodded. "Good come on then let's go", and with that they made their way downstairs and into the library.

"Now where is it?" Dad said the words automatically as he moved across the room to the bookcase where he'd replaced the old book. "Oh here it is. Now be very careful with this Kitty", he added as he handed the book over. "It's quite old and some of the pages are a bit loose so please do be careful and look after it. When you've finished with it put it back here on the shelf where I've just taken it from. It's not ours so we must treat it with respect", he admonished them all, then playfully ruffling Sam's hair, left them sitting around a little table poring over the old black book.

Chapter 5

Quickly the children rifled through the book looking for maps. There were quite a few and as they came across each one they exclaimed and gasped, fingers pointing at buildings and coastal outlines. The maps were all related to the particular part of the country they were in but of course, there were any number of bays around the coast and the book covered quite a wide area. Each time they came across another map they tried as hard as they could to relate it to their memory of the treasure map they had found. Then quickly discounted them one by one because they didn't fit; didn't seem to have buildings in the right places or didn't have the same sort of rounded bay that the coastline in their map had shown. Pretty soon, they started to become a little bit frustrated and squabbled.

"Oh come on Kitty turn the page it's not that one", Sam said with some disgust. "This is hopeless none of these seem to match at all. I mean we've already looked at half a dozen there can't be many more left. I mean how many bays can there be in this area anyway?"

"Well have you got any better ideas Sam?" Kitty retorted, "Just be a little patient. That's your trouble you know, you won't spend any time, and you expect everything to happen as soon as you want it to. Well life isn't like that. Now be quiet and let's do this properly."

Kitty was just as frustrated as Sam but now out of pique started to take an exaggeratedly long look at the map she was on, which made Sam really cross. He jumped up from the table and stumped around groaning and moaning about 'Girls, who do they think they are? Don't know anything just get in the way'. He flung himself around the room until he ended up standing by the bookcase from which Dad had taken the book.

"I'll see if there are any more books here with maps in", he said. Kitty simply grunted and continued to pore over the map even though she had already discounted it in her own mind as not being anything like the piece of coastline they were attempting to find. She was upset and frustrated and was simply being awkward while Josey was becoming increasingly bored and was settling comfortably back in her chair feeling quite drowsy. Sam started idly looking through the bookshelf when suddenly he exclaimed, "What a minute, what's this? Look, you two, look what I've found. It must have fallen out of the book. Dad said there were some loose pages. Well he was right and look here's another map and it looks just like our map." Quickly he hurried over to the table and placed the page down squarely in front of the two girls. "Look it's just the same, see!" Sam exclaimed face flushed with excitement.

"Yes Sam you're right." Kitty had forgotten her bad mood and Josey quickly sat up in her chair all thought of sleep banished from her mind. "Yes" she cried. "Look there's the building set a little way apart from the others just as in our map and the coastline is just the same and there's the little river running down to the beach. It's the same. It's the same. Now where is it?"

Of course, at that they all turned to each other and looked down at the map, no place name. Nothing written on it at all. Nothing on the other side. No way to tell where it was.

"Oh no!" Sam groaned. "It doesn't say where it is." He slumped down into a chair and put his head in his hands.

Tears filled Kitty's eyes as her frustration spilled over and she closed the book with a thump. "I'm going to ask Dad to get us a drink. We need a little time to think this through. Anyone else want one?"

Yes please", said Josey jumping to her feet and clutching Kitty's hand in hers, as much to support herself as to comfort Kitty.

"Yeh! I'll have one too", said Sam with his chin in his hand. "You two go ahead I'll put the book back and join you in a minute. You know Dad said we should look after it. I'll have a lemonade. Please." he added as an afterthought.

The two girls didn't argue but walked out of the library hand in hand to find Dad and Mum in the bar.

Sam picked up the book and the loose sheet of paper containing the map. He thought that he really ought to place the sheet back in the book before putting it back on the shelf. It was as if a light had switched on in Sam's brain. "Of course", he said, "If I find the place in the book where the map came from I'll be able to read about the map on the surrounding pages. Why didn't I think of that before?" Mentally he kicked himself, and in great excitement picked up the map and the book and began painstakingly to go through the book looking for where the map should have been located. The pages in the book were numbered of course but not the pages containing the hand drawn maps. They were printed on one side only and Sam noticed that this meant that the pages on either side took account of the map pages so that there was a gap in the numbering.

Page 29 contained text. What would have been numbered page 30 contained a map and page 31 contained a continuation of the text. Eagerly he thumbed through the pages looking for a gap in the numbering that wasn't already filled with a page containing a map. Half way through the book, he found it. He fitted the map page in the book his hands shaking with excitement. It fitted! Wowee!

Quickly, Sam scanned the pages either side of the map. He couldn't believe it. It was this hotel, the very one they were staying in. That was why it was set a little apart from the other buildings because it was up on the cliff and when the map was first drawn, it had been the only building on the cliff. Of course, they hadn't been able to tell from just looking at the map that it was a cliff at all, it just looked all flat, but the text in the book relating to the map described the hotel and even named it correctly although with a bit of a funny spelling. It was spelt 'Olde Shippe Inne' in the book but the sign, hanging outside the hotel said, 'Old Ship Inn'. "Well that must be Old English", Sam thought to himself, "And the hotel has changed shape over the years because of all the extensions that had been built. It looks like what's on our map is just the original part of the building. Reception and the main staircase."

Sam jumped up all bustle, determined that he would get the girls and prove to them once and for all, what a clever fellow he was. That would be one in the eye for Kitty she always thought she was so clever. Well he'd solved this little problem all by himself. With these thoughts and clutching the book firmly under his arm, he strode out of the library and marched firmly into the bar where Dad, Kitty and Josey had just started to play a game of 'Beat Your Neighbours Out of Doors'. This was a favourite card game of theirs either that or 'Rummy' and Dad often played with the children while Mum sat and read a book.

"Hello Sam", Dad called as Sam sauntered into the bar looking very pleased with himself, "Want to join in the game?"

"No thanks Dad", Sam replied, "I'm just reading through this book, it's very interesting and full of old maps just like you said", Sam added with a meaningful look at the girls. "I found an old map laying on the bookshelf that had fallen out of this book. It's a map of this bay and of this hotel as it was over 200 years ago." Sam was triumphant.

Both girls looked up quickly and Kitty said admiringly, "Oh have you Sam? Well done. Oh, do let's have a look. You don't mind Dad do you if we finish this game later?"

"Not at all", came the reply. "It'll give me a chance to have a rest and a read of my newspaper. Now if you three are going to make a noise I suggest you take yourselves off somewhere and don't be too long. It's now half past eight, I'll come and find you in another half an hour because it'll be time for bed."

"Oh Dad!" came the automatic groans from the children. It wouldn't have mattered what time Dad had said they must go to bed they would still have groaned. They simply didn't understand it, when they were tired in the morning they had to get up and when they were wide awake in the evening they had to go to bed. It was one of those inexplicable rules that grown ups used to make their lives uncomfortable.

"Now no groaning and think yourselves lucky to be allowed to stay up until 9 o'clock", Dad laughed. "Now off you go and don't forget 30 minutes and I shall come and find you."

"OK Dad", Sam muttered. "We'll go to my room and look at the book. Come on girls let's go." The three children scurried from the room, leaving Dad to pick up the cards that were scattered across the low drinks table.

"I wonder what those three are up to", Dad murmured.

"What's that dear?" Mum murmured still deep in her book.

"Oh nothing", Dad replied. "They just didn't protest as much as normal when I told them bedtime in thirty minutes and they left the card game. It's just unusual. Still, no doubt we'll find out soon enough. For the moment I'm just glad to have a half an hour of peace and quiet." Dad settled down with his newspaper for a quiet read.

The three children quickly scampered up the stairs to Sam's room where he immediately fished out the map from under the wardrobe where he'd left it and joined Kitty and Josey who were eagerly sitting in the middle of Sam's bed.

"OK. Gently now Sam get the map out and let's compare it to this one in the book", Kitty instructed in her bossiest manner trying to recover the initiative after Sam had been so clever.

"Can't you see that's what I'm doing Kitty? Stop being so bossy all the time. I'm the one who found the map in the book and I'm the one who found the map in the trunk in the attic", Sam complained loudly. "So if anyone should be bossy it should be me, not you."

"Oh come on you two", Josey intervened once again. "The important thing is that we've got this great clue. Come on now Sam let's all have a look and see where it leads."

Sam recovered the old map from the old wallet and very carefully unfolded it across the bed while Kitty took the book and opened it at the page Sam had found. They all sat there on the bed staring at the two maps.

"They're the same!" Josey exclaimed. "Look there's the building, there's the sea and the bay's the same shape. These other buildings are all in the same position. It's got to be the same place." Josey was very excited now. "Come on Kitty read what the book says. Does it say what this building is? The one that's got the little line coming from it on our map?"

Kitty read feverishly half-mumbling words and she skipped through the paragraphs associated with this particular map.

"Chandlers, Sail Makers, Bakers, Butchers, Stables", Kitty was naming buildings and pointing to them on the map as she went. Suddenly, she cried out, "Yes here it is. Here, this building", and she was pointing excitedly now. "This building is the 'Olde Shippe Inne'. You're right Sam, that's here, this building, this hotel where we're staying!"

The children all sat back on their haunches and looked at each other in open-mouthed amazement. Eventually Josey said in quite a small voice, "Well now we've found out where it is all we have to do is find out what that is." She traced with her finger the small line on the Treasure Map that ran from the building down towards the sea.

"It could be a road or a path I suppose", Sam said quickly, "But I reckon it must be a tunnel of some sort."

"Oh do you think so?" Josey was very excited.

"Why don't we get an up to date map and compare it with this one. If it was a road or a path then chances are, it'll still be there. I can't imagine anyone building over the top of a road. Let's go back to the library and find an Ordnance Survey map of the area. I'm sure I saw one when we were in there earlier with Dad." Kitty once again put forward a practical suggestion.

"Good idea Kitty." Sam had completely forgotten his anger now in the excitement of finding out that this very hotel was the one in his Treasure Map. "Why don't we go and get it now? Oh no, hang on a moment. Dad will be coming up any time now to make us go to bed. Why don't you go to the library and find the Ordnance Survey map Kitty while Josey and I go back to the bar to tell Mum and Dad we're going to bed, then once they think we're safely tucked up I'll come along to your bedroom and we'll compare the two maps and decide or our next course of action".

The girls readily agreed and after Sam had carefully tucked the Treasure Map back in the wallet and stowed it away under the wardrobe once more they all trooped down the stairs, Kitty to return the book to the library and to find an Ordnance Survey map, and Sam and Josey to the bar to say goodnight to their parents.

To say that Mum and Dad were surprised to find their children actually wanting to go to bed was an understatement. Dad was suspicious and Mum readily excused them as being tired out from the day and admonished her husband for 'Looking a gift horse in the mouth' as the saying goes. Come what may Dad led the children back upstairs; made sure they had cleaned their teeth and were all safely tucked up in bed before he made his way back downstairs to the bar for a 'nightcap' with his wife.

"Well let's hope that tomorrow really does finally bring some dry weather", he said as he sipped his drink. "Finally we'll be able to get outside and have some fun. I'm going to keep my eye on the kids though it seems very unusual for them to go off to bed so meekly. No fuss. I really don't understand it and when I offered to read Josey a story, she said no thanks because she was tired and wanted to go to sleep. Very odd."

"Oh do stop fussing", his wife replied. "They're fine, just tired out, stop worrying and relax." She fondly took him by the hand and they made their way upstairs stopping by Sam's door to call goodnight and the same at Kitty and Josey's door as well.

As soon as Sam had heard his parents walk past his door and had called his goodnights, he quickly slipped out of bed and retrieved the Treasure Map from under the wardrobe. Putting on his dressing gown and armed with a torch, he made his way down the corridor to his sisters' bedroom. A furtive tap on the door was answered very quickly by shuffling feet and Josey quietly opening the door for him to enter. Shushing each other and trying hard not to giggle they all perched themselves on Kitty's bed turned on their torches spreading the Treasure Map and the Ordnance Survey maps open ready to make the comparison.

"OK let's find this hotel on the Ordnance Survey map", Kitty said with authority and she proceeded to open the big map and fold it down so that only the bit they needed to see was visible. Scanning the map under the wavering light of the torches, she quickly located the Old Ship Inn and carefully they positioned the maps side by side aligning the North South directions and Sam leaned across and moved his finger across the Ordnance Survey map in the same position as the line on the Treasure Map. Interestingly they saw that once they had the maps aligned the position of the supposed road or tunnel actually lead away from the hotel towards the lower part of the cliff on which it was built. There were no buildings over it so it could indeed have been a road or path.

"There certainly isn't a road going that way", Kitty mused, "And I don't remember seeing a path either. It's all just bits of grass covering the cliff. There's nothing there at all."

"Then it must be a tunnel", Josey whispered looking from one to the other of her siblings with big, round, solemn, green eyes.

"I think you're right Josey", Kitty said after a short pause. "But I think in the morning we'd better check it out properly, perhaps when we go down to the beach we'll be able persuade Mum and Dad to go in that direction and we could search the cliff to see if there's a spot that looks like it could be the other end of a tunnel."

"Great idea Kitty", Sam whispered. "If it is a tunnel and that looks most likely then it'd have to come out somewhere at the bottom of the cliff I mean it stands to reason doesn't it?" he exclaimed with a lift of his voice and his eyebrows seeking the girl's agreement.

They all agreed that was a very good plan and that they'd suggest at breakfast the following morning they should head in that direction.

"Now", said Sam, "I'd better head off to bed and we'll all get some sleep before morning. Looks like we're going to have a very busy day."

"I thought we were all going to sleep together?" Josey was a little alarmed.

Sam laughed saying, "Don't worry Josey if a ghost comes to haunt me I'll slice it in two with my cutlass. I'd never get any sleep here with you two tossing and turning." Sliding from the bed he carefully refolded the Treasure Map, slotted it back into the wallet and bidding his sisters a whispered, "Goodnight", he silently tiptoed out of the bedroom, down the corridor to his own room. Once there he restored the map to its hiding place under the wardrobe and pulling off his dressing gown crept into bed and switched off his torch. He was so excited that he thought he would never be able to get to sleep. Thoughts of treasure and tunnels and pirates and ghostly arms invaded his thoughts but very soon, he simply drifted off to sleep with his arms flung wide and the unlit torch still clutched firmly in his out flung hand.

As Sam slept, the old hotel settled itself comfortably around him creaking and groaning slightly in the wind, the way that old buildings always do. Sometime later Sam was woken by a tapping sound. He turned over in bed and rubbed his eyes and listened, yes there it was again tap,

tap, tapping at the window. How could there be tapping at the window, his bedroom was on the second floor and there were no trees close to the hotel. He sat up in bed to get a closer look. As the covers fell from his shoulders he realised how cold it had become, it was freezing! He'd never known it to be this cold and it was August, the middle of summer. He started to get out of bed when the hairs on the back of his neck suddenly stood on end and a ghostly voice started to chant the rhyme that the children had found in the waxed wallet.

Billy Bones will have his say
That Treasure is where ye find it
Where dead men's eyes stare up and pray
Beneath the rocks ye'll find it

Now ye've got the treasure map
T'is in ye'r hands this day
There may be more than one mishap
Afore you end the play

The tunnel's hidden. Ye must take care
My treasure it be waiting
Down in the depths, beware, beware
Straight down below with Satan

Look to the window up on high
Ye see the gleaming gold
It's there ye see, tho' times gone by
Ye have to, must be bold

Now I will come and spike your gun
I must be here it seems
Until the treasure it be gone
To feed some poor man's dreams

For this I tell ye mortal fool
I hid it good, and well
The bones of my old faithful crew
Still guard it now, farewell

It was a harsh voice, a man's voice rough and low with a thick burr. Sam found himself shaking and shivering as he sat there listening to the rhyme, he wanted to call out but couldn't, his tongue seemed to have doubled in size and there was no saliva in his mouth. He sat there with his mouth working trying to shout out to Kitty and Josey but was unable to utter a sound. When the rhyme had come to an end, everything was horribly quiet and still and then suddenly Sam saw a hand move through the windowpane, without breaking the glass, it just came straight through as if the glass wasn't there. It was a big hand and deathly pale but shining with an eerie, ghostly light. It was clutching a cutlass, pale and yellow, luminous, glowing very slightly but with enough light for Sam to see the wrist was cloaked in what looked to be the cuff of a blue frock coat. Only the wrist was visible, the arm was not there, the forearm just sort of faded as it left the wrist. The hand itself was gnarled, creased and very hairy, with thick fingers and thumbs, the knuckles white where the hand gripped the sword hilt so fiercely. The fingernails were dirty, black and torn. Sam was scared, very scared, more scared than he had ever been in his life. He sat there shaking and trying to call out or even move anything just to take some action. The cutlass swivelled in the hand; the point facing directly towards Sam. It flew through the air inches past Sam's jaw, so fast he felt the rush of air and the chill made him shudder. The cutlass buried itself in the wall behind his head and as it disappeared from view a terrible low chuckle, followed by a moan, which sounded as if it had come from the very depths of hell, echoed around the room.

As soon as the cutlass had disappeared into the wall, the cold hand of panic released Sam from its grip and he fell forward on his face in the middle of the bed. He was sweating, burning hot and terribly cold all at the same time. He fell off the bed and stumbled on wobbly legs to the door, down the hall to the girl's room. He fell through the door and onto their bed as if he had just run a marathon with the very devil behind him.

The girls grumbled and moaned at him for having woken them, until that is, they realised that it wasn't one of Sam's pranks. When he had recovered and they'd fetched him a drink and he'd snuggled down between them to stop the uncontrollable shivering, he finally told them what had happened. The girls thought he was very brave to have stayed in the room and Sam didn't quite like to tell them that he hadn't actually been able to move a muscle throughout the whole experience. He simply pretended that he had been brave and hadn't allowed the ghost to frighten him. They agreed that they must now be very careful, very careful indeed. This was now very real, no longer a fairy story. They all now believed whole-heartedly that there really was a treasure and Captain Billy while undoubtedly dead was probably even more dangerous now than he had been alive. They resolved to be careful but still not to tell their parents.

"After all they probably wouldn't believe us anyway," Kitty said. "No we must find the tunnel and then the treasure and once we've got it in our hands we'll take it to Mum and Dad and won't they be surprised".

Kitty and Josey felt very excited at the prospect, for them the haunting by Cap'n Billy only served to make them absolutely convinced of his existence. Poor Sam tried to be brave but was seriously shaken by it all and had to be persuaded that he must go back to his own room or be in trouble with Mum and Dad. Eventually Kitty said that she would go down the corridor with him and take him back to his room. Then just as they were going out of the door, she stopped and begged Josey to go with her so that she wouldn't have to walk back by herself. Josey for her part was extremely glad to go because she hadn't much liked the thought of staying behind on her own anyway.

Finally, they fell asleep and in the morning when they woke, they had to convince each other that it wasn't a dream. The girls were up first and having washed, cleaned their teeth and dressed they rushed down the corridor to Sam's room, where they found him on his hands and knees scrabbling under the wardrobe trying to fish out the map which he had managed to knock back to the skirting.

"I was just making sure that it's still here", said Sam, "But I've pushed it back too far. Have you got anything long we can use to drag it out again?"

Kitty found a coat hanger in the wardrobe and managed to hook the map with the end of it and get it out. Just as they had sat down on the bed and were about to study it again, Dad opened the door and came in saying, "Come on slow coaches by the time you're ready the tide will be full and we'll not get down to the beach. I've already been down in to the town to get myself a newspaper. Come on hurry up Mum's already at breakfast and is waiting for us to join her."

"OK Dad just coming", Sam said leaning casually across the bed to hide the precious map from his gaze. "Come on girls I've just got to put some of my things away, you go with Dad and I'll come along directly."

Kitty seeing what Sam was up to, immediately jumped up pulled Josey to her feet and taking Dad's hand in hers, she pulled them both out of the room to allow Sam to refold the map and place it back in its hiding place under the wardrobe. Having competed the task Sam scurried down the corridor after them, catching them just before they reached the foot of the stairs. Playfully he jumped the last couple of steps and flung his arms around Dad's neck holding on tightly and grabbing a quick 'piggy back'.

"Whoa there Sam you're choking me", Dad spluttered staggering backwards and pushing Sam off. "Don't damage the goods. We've got a lot of things to enjoy today. Now come on all of you let's go and eat some nice eggs, bacon and sausage."

Chapter 6

In the dining room, where Mum was waiting, breakfast was already on the table.

"We thought we'd have a nice cooked breakfast today", said Mum after giving them all a once over and a kiss on the cheek.

The children sat down; smiled at their parents and tucked in to a hearty breakfast of fried eggs, sausages, bacon and baked beans with toast and marmalade on the side. Sam loved sausages while Josey was very keen on fried eggs, so they swapped, making sure that Mrs Franklyn didn't see them.

Kitty was determined to try to make sure that Dad and Mum would take them to the beach in the direction of the line on the map, or the tunnel as they now thought of it, took.

"Which part of the beach are we going to today Dad?" she enquired in her most interested tone. "Perhaps we could go down the cliff path outside the hotel? There might be some really, good rock pools down by the base of the cliff. I had a look out of the window earlier and it doesn't look like it's too steep and it would save us walking into town and there won't be as many people around."

"Yes OK Kitty", Dad replied quite amused. "We can go down there first and have a look if it's no good we'll move on. What do you think darling?" he said turning to Mum.

"Well it's alright with me", Mum joined the conversation, "You know how much I enjoy rock pools and catching little fish, crabs, prawns and starfish. But if it's too steep we'll have to go somewhere else."

"Oh I'm sure it won't be", Kitty quickly replied. "And we'll help carry everything", Sam joined in quickly understanding exactly what Kitty was up to.

"Well that'll be a first!" Dad exclaimed. "I'll hold you to that Sam and no moaning half way down and expecting me to carry everything."

Sam looked a bit sheepish but Josey joined in adding, "I'll carry my share too, after all I'm quite grown up now and I'm quite strong too."

"Certainly strong enough to carry a bag or a chair", Mum agreed. "Well come on then finish your breakfasts and then up stairs to get whatever it is you want to take to the beach."

"Bring the kite Sam. We'll see just how high it'll fly. If we can get it to fly above the height of the cliff it should soar away and we'll have some fun trying to loop the loop with it", Dad laughed. "We'll see how many seagulls we can knock out of the air."

"You will not!" Mum squawked, flicking her napkin at her husband and laughing along with them. "Come on now let's go. See you back downstairs in five minutes."

The family pushed back their chairs laughing and joking with each other. Dad chased the children out of the dining room and up the stairs while Mum brought up the rear. With raised eyebrows, she admonished her husband.

"Really you're as bad as the children. How many times have I told not to run indoors?"

A few minutes later, they were back downstairs, the children clutching nets, spades and buckets, while Mum and Dad had an assortment of towels, chairs and bags full of interesting things to nibble on when they got to the beach.

"Right now you lot everyone take a bag, a chair or a towel", Dad bellowed above the noise as he tried to usher the children out of the hotel before any of the other guests made a complaint that they were simply being too noisy.

Of course, the children all picked the smallest, lightest thing they could and ran off down the steps making their way to the cliff path. "Hoi, you lot", Dad called after them but too late they were gone with Mum quickly following. Dad looked askance at the mound of bags and paraphernalia that had been left on the ground at his feet. "How on earth am I ever going to get this lot down to the beach?" he grumbled to himself. "I'll have a heart attack on the way down that'll teach them." With a sigh, he loaded up the bags and struggled after his family bumping chairs and bags against what would become quite sore knees by the time he managed to get to the beach.

The children had run on ahead with Kitty leading the way. They followed the path, which led down to the beach. It wound its way backwards and forwards, as to go straight down would have been far too steep. As they ran and stumbled down the path Kitty kept turning back to look at the hotel, trying to calculate in her mind quite where the tunnel came from and went to.

It was very difficult to estimate where the tunnel was in relation to the cliff path. Kitty knew that the tunnel eventually made its way to the sea somewhere but couldn't quite get in her mind the geography of it. The cliff path lead down and around one side of the cliff straight onto the beach. Once it had left the cliff, it was sand and pebbles more or less all the way. Kitty didn't believe that a tunnel could possibly exist in sand. She had experience of building tunnels in sand.

The year before when the family had been on holiday at a different coastal resort they had been on the beach and the children decided that if they made two large castles with moats, towers and turrets they could join them together with a large tunnel that would link the moats of the castles. They had made the two castles with their moats but no matter how deeply they dug between the two castles or how hard they tried the tunnel kept collapsing. Dad had explained that tunnels built in sand would collapse, as the grains were too small and kept shifting as the wind blew and the sand moved at even the slightest step.

"No", she thought, "The tunnel can't follow the beach path. It has to be higher up, dug through the cliff itself then it must come out at the bottom somewhere near the sea." She talked with Josey and Sam as they ran along together and explained her thinking. The other two agreed and when they got to the beach Kitty said, "Let's make sure that Mum and Dad set up camp somewhere this side of the cliff so that we can go exploring around the front and the other side without them seeing us." She chose a nice sheltered spot in between two big boulders or bits of cliff as they were, which stuck out of the beach like the backs of big blue whales swimming in a sea of sand.

"Here we are Mum this'll be a nice place to put our stuff. If the wind blows up we'll get some protection behind these bits of cliff", she said as Mum came trudging across the sand with Dad stumbling along behind her. "Come and give me a hand you rotten lot", he called. "You all ran off and left me to carry half the hotel."

The children giggling and laughing, ran across the sand, and relieved him of some of the bags and chairs and carried them back to Mum, who was already engrossed in a nearby rock pool.

The chairs and bags were dropped in a big heap and the children ran off across the beach while their long-suffering Dad started to set up the chairs and place the bags in a more orderly fashion. All he wanted was to sit down, pour himself a cup of coffee from the flask and have a relaxing read of his newspaper.

As soon as the children were out of earshot, Kitty started to tell the others all about her idea. "If you look back up at the cliff you can just see the rooftop of our hotel", Kitty explained. "There, just there, beyond that big tree. You can just see the red tiles of the hotel roof and the clock tower beyond". The children squinted and peered and eventually they could all see where Kitty was pointing. They all took a good, hard, long look at the landscape between the beach and the top of the cliff where the hotel was situated. They all agreed with Kitty that the cliff path couldn't possibly be the route of the tunnel. No it had to be somewhere else in the cliff but where?

They scanned the side of the cliff looking for anything that might mark the course of the tunnel but nothing showed up, nothing that even looked a remote possibility. After a while, Sam suggested that they should move closer to the base of the cliff and look to see if they could locate the other end of the tunnel. "After all", he said, "The tunnel has got to come out somewhere. It must end up in a cave or something at the base of the cliff".

The girls thought this was a very good suggestion so they picked up their buckets and spades and made their way across the sand to the base of the cliff. Unfortunately, the tide was only just on the ebb, it having been high tide at the time they were having breakfast, so at this moment a large part of the cliff was still under water. However, the children started at the top of the beach and by clambering over the rocks and through the rock pools, started working their way down towards the water. They checked along the base of the cliff and peered in at every nook and cranny, because as Sam said, "We don't know how big the opening is do we? And anyway there might be a secret entrance with a big rock in front of it or something".

As you might have guessed the children found nothing big enough even for them to squeeze through let alone a man as big as Cap'n Billy must have been. After a while, feeling extremely frustrated and not a little bored Josey gave up and started to fish in the rock pools instead. She managed to capture a small crab and got really quite excited, so much so, that Kitty and Sam joined her and they all fished for a while, paddling through the rock pools and dipping their nets in anywhere that looked a likely spot. Mum came over with their swimming costumes saying, "Come on you three change into these before you all get your clothes soaking wet".

The children changed one at a time behind a big towel held out by Mum. Then they all joined in the hunt and caught a few more little crabs, some long silver fish, which they couldn't name and a few tiny shrimps, all of which they took back in buckets and showed very proudly to Dad, who showed a lot more enthusiasm than he actually felt as he'd been interrupted half way through the crossword.

Mum and the girls knelt around the buckets watching the antics of the little fish and crabs in apparently endless fascination. Dad and Sam however were soon bored with this and Dad searched through the pile of stuff he had carried to the beach and extracted a very large kite, which he, with the aid of Sam, now proceeded to put together. The wind was blowing quite hard now from landward towards the sea.

"Come on Sam. Let's see how high we can get this thing to go", Dad laughed as he pulled Sam to his feet.

It was one of those stunt kites where there are two strings attached one either side of the kite, pull one string the kite dips that way and pull the other it goes back up again. The difficulty with that type of kite is that it sometimes flies round in a series of circles and you have to be very clever to make it go back the other way to untangle the strings. Never the less it was fun and the wind was blowing quite strongly now.

Dad sent Sam off down the beach towards the water while he held the strings one in either hand. When Sam was some good distance away Dad shouted, "OK let her go!" Sam threw the kite in the air and immediately the wind caught it and up she went soaring into the sky. Dad let out more string evenly from either hand and the kite, pulling and tugging like some demented demon roared higher and higher into the sky, making an awful lot of noise as the wind screeched through the flapping wings. Sam ran back up the beach and the three children jumped around shrieking whooping as the kite dived and bucked in response to the sharp tugs Dad gave on either string.

"My go! My go!" Sam shouted and Dad carefully handed the strings to Sam and stood back to watch. The wind was so fierce that Sam was very nearly pulled off his feet but he steadied himself, planted his feet firmly in the sand and proceeded to experiment with the handling of the kite by pulling first one string then the other. Of course, it wasn't long before the strings became hopelessly tangled and the kite crashed to the ground with a resounding thump! This time Josey went running down the beach to pick up the kite while Kitty took up the strings. Dad walked along the line of the strings and untangled them, Josey then threw the kite in the air and it was Kitty's turn to feel the power of the wind tugging at the kite strings.

Sam had wandered off back to the rock pools feeling slightly aggrieved from the mickey taking he had suffered when the kite had crashed to the floor. The tide had gone out quite a way by now and the tops of some of the bigger rocks that lay some way from the bottom of the cliff and were usually completely covered by the sea, were sitting there with their tops just out of the water. It was by now almost low tide. Sam wandered down the beach. It shelved quite quickly as it moved away from the cliff and he paddled out as far as he could towards the exposed rocks.

Sam decided he would swim out and perch on top of the rocks; that would show his sisters. Show them what, he wasn't quite sure but he was still smarting from the catcalls and jeers that had come his way when the kite crashed into the sand. He splashed out up to his waist then kicked off from the bottom and swam the 5 metres that took him to the first rock. Once there he grabbed hold and hauled himself up the side and stood on top calling and jeering to his family. The girls immediately lost interest in the kite and ran towards him leaving Dad to pull the kite down and pack it away.

Once they reached the water Kitty and Josey quickly jumped in and started swimming towards Sam. Kitty, who was by far the stronger swimmer reached him first and hauled herself up on top of the rock and settled herself to help Josey out of the water. Josey was by now laying on her back and paddling fiercely with her arms and legs. She was a competent swimmer but tired very easily and tended just to paddle around. Josey liked snorkelling because that suited her swimming style; paddling around in the shallows is what she liked to do. However, she made the rock quite easily, turned over and trod water holding her hands up to Kitty and Sam to pull her onto the rock. They duly obliged and soon all three of them were jumping up and down calling to Mum and Dad and feeling quite the little explorers.

After a while, they sat and looked down into the sea marvelling at the rush and whoosh as the currents broke and eddied around the rocks. They couldn't possibly have swum between the rocks, the sea simply poured through in a great torrent, they'd have been dashed up against the great boulders and suffered serious injury if they'd tried. Looking down they saw that what they had thought were two individual boulders at the end of a cascade of smaller rocks were in fact simply part of the cliff itself. Looking back from this vantage point it was obvious that here the cliff had spilled out into the sea and been mostly covered by the sand so that it appeared as if these two rocks were isolated. However, from here they could see the different shadows and shapes made by the rock that lay under the water. This was almost like a tunnel heading down from the cliff right into the water! Try as they might the children couldn't see far enough under the water to see if there was an entrance between the two big boulders. The sea, even though it wasn't very rough today, had stirred up enough sand and mud to be cloudy and the visibility was very poor but my goodness weren't they excited!

"This has to be the other end of the tunnel we saw in the map. It just has to be!" Sam cried, over and over again, "Oh how can we get down to see if there's an entrance", but of course they couldn't and besides Mum and Dad had begun to call them back again as they were concerned that the children might be in some danger sitting there on the rocks with the waves breaking over them. Quickly they dived off the rock into the sea, swimming to the shore where Dad was waiting for them with a towel each to drape around their shoulders.

While they had been on the rocks, the sun had gone in and dark clouds had gathered away to the west, a chill had descended up on the beach and the children realised that it had become quite cold with the threat of rain not very far away. The whole family rushed to get dressed and pack up their things before the rain came. While they were dressing Kitty stared out to where the rocks were, trying to memorise their position in relation to the base of the cliff and to pinpoint in her mind just where the shadows in the water seemed to indicate the position of the tunnel against the backdrop of the cliff. It was difficult to make that sort of judgement from the beach.

"What time does the tide go fully out, Dad", she asked, "and how far out does it go? I'd quite like to explore around the base of the cliff and those rocks we were sitting on when the sea isn't there".

"I think low tide is about 3 o'clock this afternoon, if I remember the tide chart correctly and it would be interesting to see quite how far the tide goes out, although I don't think it goes out very much further than it is now. If it's not raining, we'll come back after lunch and take a look. You saw didn't you when you swam out, that the beach shelves quite steeply about 10 metres out? Well you remember that I told you I found a book in the hotel library that talked about the history of this place. One of the chapters was about this bay and what it used to look like a couple of centuries ago. It wasn't very much like it is now at all. It used to be quite a big beach that sloped gently down to the sea. It was used to beach the local fishing fleet when they wanted to do any work on the boats. Over the years, there has been lots of erosion around this coast. A couple of hundred years ago the cliff itself was much further out to sea. Almost 25 metres of the cliff have disappeared in the last 50 years alone. It's just fallen into the sea and been washed away. In addition, there has been a lot of landslip and the currents have changed making the sea come much further up the beach than it ever did before. The local council bring sand and gravel here every year to make up the beach and keep us tourists happy, otherwise, there wouldn't be much of anything left. However, they do a good job don't they? It is a nice beach still and it attracts families like us, who like nothing better than making sandcastles and rock pooling. Now come on the three of you or we're going to get very wet indeed!"

The three children gave each other very significant looks. They hadn't thought that the beach could possibly have changed that much since the map was first drawn by Cap'n Billy. On the way back to the hotel, the children walked quickly ahead of their Mum and Dad and Kitty said in a low whisper, "Well, that might explain a great deal. I guess that when bits of the cliff were washed away, it was only the upper part, the mud and loose stones and dirt. The rocks we saw at the bottom and where we swam out to must be the remains of the original cliff that have been uncovered by the erosion that happens here year after year. I bet our tunnel goes down through the cliff and ends somewhere near where we swam. When the tide goes out, I'm sure we'll find an opening down there between the two large rocks. When we come back down again after lunch, we'll have to try to get Dad to let us go down there and explore. I just hope the tide goes out far enough for us to be able to explore around those rocks properly."

Josey and Sam nodded their agreement and they all hurried on to the hotel as quickly as they could to avoid the rain, which had just started to fall. Reaching the hotel Mum and Dad told them to go upstairs, take a shower and wash their hair. "You've got to get all the salt off left behind by the sea water otherwise you'll never be able to drag a comb through your hair and it'll make you itch", Mum had said with some emphasis.

"And change into something warm", Dad added as he handed them their towels. "See you back downstairs in half an hour", he called to them as they raced up the stairs.

"OK Sam", said Kitty taking charge again. "You come along to our room as soon as you've finished and got changed. Then we'll decide upon our plan of action. And make sure you knock before you come in!" she added quickly. Kitty had just reached the age where she didn't like to be seen by boys, not even her brother, unless she was properly dressed.

"OK. OK." Sam mumbled as he stumped off down the corridor to his own room. Sam found it a little irksome to always be told what to do by his big sister. The problem was he didn't have any better suggestions and Kitty always seemed to come up with the ideas first.

The girls ran down the corridor to their own room and fell inside pulling off their clothes and turning on the shower. Kitty went first, she was determined she was definitely not going to be in the shower when Sam arrived. The girls chatted excitedly to each other while they were showering going over the morning's events and discussing what they should do next.

Chapter 7

A matter of some ten minutes later the girls' bedroom door was flung open wide and Sam came quickly into the room. His hair was wet and hastily brushed with what can only have been his fingers. His choice of clothes would have done justice to a colour-blind tramp, black jeans, orange socks and a green t-shirt.

"Oh Sam!" Kitty shrieked pulling on her trousers very quickly. "Why on earth can't you knock before you come in? Really!" she added in despair, "Who on earth would want a brother like you?"

"Well nobody would want a sister like you, that's for certain", Sam shouted back turning to go.

"Hold on Sam", Josey grabbed him by the arm dragging him back into the room. "Come on you two stop arguing all the time we've got some serious planning to do now and not much time before we have to go down for lunch. I told you Sam would be along soon Kitty you should've dressed more quickly and Sam you know how Kitty is, please try not to just walk in on us again. I don't know, I seem to spend all my time pulling you two apart", Josey ended in exasperation, for once seeming much older than her years.

Kitty and Sam looked sullenly at each other and then Kitty burst into laughter at the sight of Sam's clothes. "Goodness Sam. Where on earth did you get such a selection of clothes?" she giggled.

"What's wrong with them?" Sam asked in astonishment holding his arms out wide and looking down at himself.

Josey steered him across the room and stood him in front of a tall mirror hung on the front of the wardrobe. Sam looked at himself and slowly grinned his charming, winning smile. "I guess I do look a bit of a state at that", he said running his hands through his hair and trying unsuccessfully to push it into some sort of order. "And", he added, "I guess orange and green isn't too successful as a colour combination. Oh well who cares", he shrugged and turned away from the mirror sharing the girls laughter. "I'm a boy. I don't need to be colour coordinated. Now come on let's decide what we're going to do this afternoon."

"Well after we've had lunch, we've got to persuade Mum and Dad to go back down to the beach. We need to get back to those rocks we were on when the tide has gone fully out. We might then be able to see if it really is the end of our tunnel." Kitty said decisively.

Sam and Josey nodded in agreement. "I think it's stopped raining but it looks very grey still. I hope that doesn't mean we'll have to stay in", Sam said looking out of the bedroom window.

"Oh I'm sure I'll be able to persuade Dad to take us", Josey said impishly, "but we might have to leave Mum behind", she added.

"I bet Mum'll be pleased to spend an afternoon with her head buried in another book and you're right Josey, I'm sure Dad will come with us. Come on then", Kitty instructed. "We'd better get ourselves down to lunch or they'll be sending out search parties."

The children jumped up and headed downstairs where they found their parents seated at their normal table perusing the lunch menu.

"Hello you three", Dad called as they entered the dining room. "I was just about to send out a search party." The three children giggled at this giving each other shushing looks as the giggles started to turn into real laughter. "Well what on earth's the matter with you", Dad looked at them in surprise.

"Oh it's nothing Dad", said Josey dropping into the chair beside him, "It's just that Kitty had just finished saying that you would be sending out a search party."

"Oh dear am I really that predictable?" Dad said in pretend sulk. "Then I shan't worry about you ever again. Next time I shall start lunch without you then you'll get all thin and skinny", he added giving Josey's ribs a quick prod, which made her jump up from her chair in an effort to get away from his tickling fingers.

"OK. OK. Enough!" Mum intervened. "This is a dining room not a playground. Sit down Josey."

"But Dad was tickling me", Josey complained loudly.

"OK. Well Dad should know better", came the reply.

"In trouble again", Dad sighed. "Take note Sam and learn how not to handle a woman. When you do grow up and get married remember never to ask me for advice. Now let's order lunch before I get into even more trouble", he added rolling his eyes in mock exasperation while giving Josey another tickle in the ribs.

"Oh you're hopeless", Mum said giving him a broad smile. "There's fresh fish and chips on the menu shall we all have that?" she looked round the table receiving nods of agreement as she went. The waitress, who had been hovering nearby came up, wrote the order on her pad and went off into the kitchen.

"What shall we do after lunch?" Mum continued, "It looks to me very much like rain I'm afraid. Shall we all stay in the hotel and read or play games?"

"Oh No!" the children all exclaimed at once. "No Mum we've spent so much time indoors this holiday let's go out, let's go back to the beach. There are still lots of rock pools and if we take our coats it won't matter if it rains we won't get wet", Josey wheedled looking directly at her Dad. "Dad'll take us if you don't want to go. You can stay here and read if you want to but Dad will come with us won't you Dad?" she continued imploringly, hanging onto his arm and cuddling up as close as she could without actually letting her bottom leave her chair.

"Yes I don't mind", Dad shrugged, quite pleased to be cuddled, easily flattered by his youngest daughter.

"She wraps you around her little finger", Mum laughed. "Well you can all go off if you like. I shall enjoy a quiet time here in the hotel. I'm half way through a really good book and I don't much fancy wandering around in the rain. I'll see you when you get back."

The children all smiled at their parents and tucked into the fish and chips that had just been placed in front of them by a beaming waitress.

Once they'd finished they all agreed how delicious it had been. "Nothing quite like freshly caught fish", Dad had said. "I don't think I could manage a pudding after that little lot", and they all agreed. "OK come on then", he continued, "Upstairs for hats and coats and we'll get going. See you down here in five minutes", he called at their disappearing backs.

"You have a nice rest darling", he murmured to his wife giving her a quick peck on the cheek before following the children up the stairs to collect his own outdoor clothes. "We probably won't be out more than an hour or two. Whatever, we'll find you when we get back", he said as his wife disappeared in the direction of the lounge.

"Well done Jo", Sam whispered as the children sped up the stairs. "I knew you could get Dad to agree to come with us. See you downstairs in two minutes", he yelled as dived into his room to get his things.

"OK", Josey called back, feeling quite pleased with herself. Grabbing her coat and hat, she and Kitty quickly flew back down the corridor and busied themselves in the hallway putting on their Wellington boots while waiting for Dad. Sam quickly joined them and by the time Dad had made it down the stairs with his things they were already dressed and anxious to be away.

"Alright! Alright! You lot. Anyone would think you hadn't been out for centuries. If you're that eager to go just wait for me outside while I put my boots on. I won't be a minute."

The children all ran outside and across the car park to the edge of the cliff and were standing there peering over down at the beach when Dad finally came out of the front door. "Look the tide's gone out completely", Kitty was saying, "and there, just there are the two rocks we swam out to."

"But those aren't rocks", Josey replied. "They're part of the cliff. Look you can see where the rocks run all the way down the beach. It's clear now the sea has gone. The cliff sort of slopes down the beach and it's solid rock all the way down. The bit that's been washed away over the years must just have been the mud and loose stuff that was sitting on top of the real rock."

"That's right Josey", Dad said as he came up with them. "As I said before, over the centuries lots of soil and landslip has been carried away by the sea but only what would have been the topsoil and subsoil. What's left is the bedrock that formed the core of the cliff and of course you can see from here that it runs quite a long way down the beach and reaches right down to the low water mark. I'm amazed that we haven't found an old smuggler's cave. It would have been ideal for that when the beach was used for shipping back in the old days. Come on let's get down to the beach, the wind up here is whipping the rain straight into our faces and I'm getting quite cold. It'll be better down on the beach in the lee of the wind." Dad turned and trudged off in the direction of the cliff path leaving the three children looking at each other with excitement written across their faces.

"Not a word Josey", Kitty admonished, "I know you. You really want to tell Dad all about it don't you. Well not yet.

Until we find the tunnel there's nothing to tell apart from we've found a silly old fake map that might have come from any old toy box anywhere."

"Oh but that doesn't take into account the ghost of Cap'n Billy coming into my room does it?" Sam said with some feeling.

"But Dad would just say that was simply a bad dream", Kitty countered. "No we've just got to keep quiet until we've found something convincing. Now come on or Dad'll wonder what we're doing", saying that Kitty bounded away chasing after Dad with the other two at her heels.

Once down on the beach the children made straight for the two big rocks, clambering over the sand and rocks until they reached them. Looking back up the beach it was obvious where the underlying rock was, it simply fell out of the cliff about half way up and rolled down the beach to the sea in a great wide strip, looking vaguely like the back of a gigantic whale half covered by sand.

"Phew! It's really big isn't it?" Dad exclaimed as he caught up with the children and turned to look back up the beach towards the cliff. "I guess this is just about low tide and these two rocks seem to be the last line of defence." He and the children looked up at the two rocks, which towered over them perhaps four or five feet high on the landward side and eight feet high on the seaward side where the cliff ended and dropped steeply into the sea. The sea was lapping around the base of the rocks that were joined together where they abutted the cliff proper but with about five or six feet wide gap between them that could be seen from the seaward side when the children hung on and peered around the corner.

"Oh look Dad", Kitty cried, clinging on to the rock and leaning as far out as she could. "It's a sort of a cave. It's very dark in there but it seems to go back quite a long way. It's almost as if there's a tunnel leading back through the rock."

"Oh let's have a look", Sam and Josey yelled together and before Dad could stop them they both waded into the water and seemed enormously surprised when the waves lapped over the tops of their boots, wetting their trousers and socks. Josey immediately shrieked and rushed from the water clutching her father's arm in horror. "I've got wet feet now", she sobbed.

"Well that was a pretty, silly thing to do Josey", Dad replied without much sympathy. "Don't worry. You won't get into trouble and I'm sure the water isn't going to cause you any lasting damage", he added playfully. "We'll dry you out when we get back to the hotel. Mum doesn't have to know, you can just go and change and she won't be any the wiser." In truth, Dad was protecting himself as much as Josey for he was pretty sure he would get into trouble as well for not looking after the children properly and for allowing them to get wet.

Meanwhile, Sam had decided, 'In for a penny in for a pound.' Having got wet feet he thought he might just as well explore properly and so had waded a bit further into the gap or cave between the rocks.

"Be careful Sam", Dad called as Sam disappeared from view. "It's OK Dad", Sam replied. "Actually there's nothing much here apart from a load of old junk that the sea has thrown up. It's full of old beer cans, bits of wood and seaweed. As far as I can see, the cave is blocked at the back. Filled right up to the top with bits of rock and sand and rubbish. It might once have been open but it certainly isn't anymore", he added as he waded back round the rock and up onto the beach.

"Yes well, we might have expected it to be full of rubbish", Dad replied. "It has the look of what might once have been an old smuggler's cave and maybe there was once a tunnel that lead back up the beach and through the cliff to our hotel. That's just the sort of thing I've read about in old books but if ever there was a tunnel it's long since gone. Collapsed and forgotten and the hotel has changed so much over the years that any tunnel would have been built over long ago."

Dad noticed the crestfallen look that had appeared on the children's faces. "Oh I'm sorry", he said, "You really were expecting to find a tunnel weren't you? Well I'm sorry to have to tell you that really is just fiction. No doubt, there were smugglers in the old days. Indeed, we know there were but that was a couple of hundred years ago, there won't be anything left from that time I'm afraid. The sea, the wind and the weather will all have combined with the march of progress. In other words, all the building that's gone on in this area would have made sure that any old tunnels or caves had given up their secrets long ago. No treasure trove to be found today children. Now come on it's blowing quite hard now, there's more rain in the air and the sky looks dark enough for a storm. Let's get back to the hotel and dry off shall we?"

Glumly the children nodded their heads and trekked back up the beach, Josey and Sam squelching their way along and up the cliff path. At the door of the hotel Dad made them take their boots off and empty any remaining water out before they went in. He also made them take their socks off and wring them out.

"Up to your rooms now and put your socks on the radiators to dry. I'll stuff newspaper in your boots to dry them out and leave them down here in the hall. Then we'll all go and find Mum in the lounge and perhaps have a cup of tea."

"OK Dad", came the reply as the morose children shambled and slumped their way up the stairs.

The wet wellington boots were duly stuffed with old newspaper and left by the hall radiator to dry, after which, Dad made his way into the lounge where he found his wife sitting with her head buried in a book.

"Hello darling", he called. "The poor kids have just had a terrible disappointment."

"Oh what's that?" his wife enquired lifting her head from her book.

"They had convinced themselves that we'd find a smuggler's cave at the bottom of the cliff where it reaches the sea, and we might have done. It certainly looked like it could at one time or another have been a cave and maybe even a tunnel but it's completely blocked now. Full of old rubbish, sand, debris and possibly even a cave- in where the cliff and the beach has moved over the years. You should have seen their faces when we looked inside. I'm sure they thought they were going to look in and find chests full or pirate treasure", he chuckled.

"That's your fault", came the reply. "If you hadn't filled their heads with silly stories about pirates and smugglers and trotted out that old man who told them all about Cap'n Billy and his murdering crew they wouldn't even have thought of it."

"Oh come on. It was only a bit of fun. Anyway, no harm done they're OK. They'll soon find something else to think about. That's the romance of being a child you're allowed to think the unthinkable, to let your imagination rule the day. It's called fun. You're always so practical. They're just kids after all", he replied tetchily, not happy about being grumbled at by his wife who ought to be grateful that he'd taken the children off for the afternoon and allowed her some peace and quiet. The last thing he needed was to be lectured on how to keep the children happy. If it were left up to their Mum, they'd be indoors and quiet all of the time.

He was being ridiculous he knew and threw himself into a chair on the other side of the table and buried his head in a newspaper, while his wife simply shrugged her shoulders and ignored him, going gratefully back to her novel.

Chapter 8

A little while later, the children found their parents in the lounge and sagged into chairs, drawing them in to form a circle. Their faces were glum and they just slumped in the chairs and were quiet. Their Mum hardly looked up from her book but Dad put down his newspaper and said, "Oh come on now you lot. Cheer up. Just because we didn't find a pirate's tunnel there's nothing to look so fed up about. We're on holiday. We're here to have fun".

"Yes Dad", they chorused in reply but still sat looking like 'Out of work bloodhounds', one of Dad's favourite expressions. "I know. How about a cup of tea and a piece of cake?"

"Oh no! We've only just had lunch. It'll spoil their dinner", Mum admonished. Her hearing acutely tuned to any idiocy on her husband's part. Just as Dad opened his mouth to respond to this uncalled for interruption, Kitty said, "Oh it's OK Dad we're not hungry anyway. Come on you two let's go back to the library and look in those old books again. I want to find out some more about Cap'n Billy". She jumped up from her chair and exited, closely followed by Josey and Sam before their parents could really start to argue.

"Mum's no fun sometimes", Josey complained. "She's always so sensible about everything. Poor Dad must get really fed up with being told off".

"Mmmm! But Dad doesn't think things through always", Kitty replied. "Never mind. Come on let's have another go through that book we found, there might be clues we've overlooked".

The children made their way into the library, which fortunately was empty, and Sam located the book that had told them all about Cap'n Billy. He reached it down from the shelf and found the chapter they'd read before. As the children sat around the table each trying to read and reread the appropriate portions looking for something, anything they'd missed before, Mrs Franklyn walked in and said in her jolly voice "Oh hello there children. Raining again eh? I'm so sorry but there's not very much I can do about the weather. Did you find anything much up in the attic the other day? I hope you found some nice things to play with".

"Oh yes thank you", Josey replied, immediately getting up and going over to Mrs Franklyn. "We found some really nice things, thank you. I got a dolls house and Kitty got some books and Sam found an old chest full of stuff to do with the sea. It made us think of the story that old man told us the other night about smugglers and Cap'n Billy's ghost. We came here into the library to see if we could find any books about him and we have found one but it really doesn't say very much. We were hoping to find a map and perhaps a secret tunnel." Josey smiled disingenuously while the other two children smothered a gasp. "Do you know about any secret tunnels or passages in the hotel, Mrs Franklyn?" Josey went on, "This hotel seems just the sort of place where there could be one, doesn't it?" she enquired of the other two.

Mrs Franklyn laughed and ruffled Josey's hair. "Oh yes I must say it does seem just the right sort of place my dear, what with the ghost and everything and I do seem to recall some sort of old nonsense about there being some sort of secret passage or tunnel but I'm blessed if I can remember where it was or where it went to. I know old Martha has been working in this hotel for more than 70 years. She only works part time now because she must be well into her 80s. She was just a child when she first started working here but she knows everything about the hotel and the surrounding area. She's still got her marbles but doesn't get around quite as well as she used to and you're in luck because today is one of her working days. She doesn't do much any more just sort of flicks a duster here and there and does a bit of washing up but she's become a sort of fixture here and she wouldn't know what to do with herself if she didn't come in twice a week. Why don't you go down into the staff parlour and share a pot of tea with her? She'll be having a drink about now and she's always ready for a little chat. Don't tire her out too much with all your jumping around. She's a very nice old woman but a little bit deaf so speak up clearly or you'll find she's answering questions you haven't asked". Mrs Franklyn chuckled and ruffled Josey's hair again. "Get along with you now I've got things to do." Chuckling to herself, she walked out of the library in the direction of the reception area.

"Oh Josey you took an awful chance there", Kitty said in admiration, "and it worked a treat. Come on let's go down to the staff parlour and find Martha. We aren't beaten yet".

Quickly the children headed off down the back stairs to the staff parlour where they found old Martha sitting at a table with a cup of tea and a teapot in front of her.

"Oh hello", Kitty said pushing Josey in front of her. "Mrs Franklyn said we could come down here I hope you don't mind?"

"Mind? Why should I mind my dears?" the old woman replied, "Nice to have some company while I drink my tea", she continued. "Now why don't you three children sit down and join me. My, you are bonny aren't you? All blond hair and blue eyes. Are you brother and sisters?"

"Yes we are", Josey said as she plonked herself down in the chair next to Martha "And yes please we'd really like to join you if we may. My name is Josey and this is Kitty and Sam. We're staying here on holiday and we've been a bit fed up because of the weather. Mrs Franklyn said that we might come down and talk to you about when you first started working at this hotel. We've been reading all about Cap'n Billy and his smuggler gang and we sort of thought that there really must be some sort of secret passage or something left over from those days."

"Oh lor' bless you child, secret passages eh? I should guess that you're trying to find old Billy Bones' treasure is that what you're up to?" she cackled a little as she laughed. The children trying to humour her all smiled and Josey continued, "Well yes but of course we don't really expect to find any treasure it's just something to do to keep ourselves amused while it's still raining. Can you tell us anything about the hotel? Mrs Franklyn doesn't know anything but she was pretty sure that if anyone knew anything at all it would be you", Josey flattered and old Martha responded as she had hoped.

"Yes my dear, it would only be me that knew if anyone did. I've been around much longer than most and I started working here when I was only 14 years old. I was much prettier in those days and served in the bar where all the working-men used to come after work and straight from the boats, when there were boats of course. But everything changed during the war", she reminisced. "We had lots of foreigners here then, Yanks and Poles and the like. Things changed and not always for the better. After the War, all sorts of building work went on when the new owners took over. It was them that made this place into a proper hotel, before that it was just a pub with a few rooms for occasional visitors. Mind you not all the changes were bad", she went on. "They put in the first proper indoor toilets we'd had round here. People came from miles around just to have a look. Did wonders for the trade. And then of course back in the 1970's they converted all the rooms to have their own bathrooms, no more waiting in a draughty corridor for some other guest to finish having a bath. Oh I can't tell you the number of times I've come across a guest in the corridor with their legs crossed bursting to use the toilet", she chuckled gleefully at the memory and the children joined in humouring her.

"Did they do that in the old part of the hotel too?" Josey enquired trying to lead the conversation back to the tunnel, "Because we don't have a toilet in our room."

"Oh no my dear", Martha responded. "Of course they had to be careful because it's a listed building and all those planning people! Oh, they made such a fuss. Couldn't take down this wall or that; had to preserve the lathe and plaster; couldn't remove a beam or replace a lintel. I tell you it was a wonder the owners didn't just give up and go."

"But they didn't", Josey interjected again. "They got it done in the end and it's a really nice hotel now. I expect they had to do a lot of work down here and in the kitchens didn't they and what about the cellar? I expect that's where any old tunnel would have been wouldn't it?" Josey continued winning admiring glances from both Kitty and Sam.

"Oh yes they had to do a lot work down here", Martha replied. "What with all these new fangled regulations about health and safety and that EU always interfering. Why, do you know that poor old Albert Butcher had to close down his shop a few years ago because he couldn't meet the new regulations. Couldn't get a big enough cold room and didn't have the space to separate the different meats, wasn't allowed to run an abattoir from the premises". Martha seemed set to go on and on about the state of the world, in particular the state of England and the interference of the local inspectors goaded into action by the faceless bureaucrats from the European Union. The children looked at each other in despair. How on earth, could they get Martha back on the subject of secret tunnels? Josey had done her best but Martha had proved too much for even her winning ways.

Sam suddenly stood up from the table and asked very politely, "Could I pour you another cup of tea Martha or is there anything I can get you?" Martha was quite taken aback at being interrupted in such a polite manner. She looked at Sam in a curious way and said, "Why thank you young man I'd like another cup of tea. Why don't you all help yourselves to a biscuit? I'm sure Mrs Franklyn wouldn't mind. I do run on a bit I know", she added.

"That's very kind of you", Kitty replied on behalf of everyone, taking her cue from Sam she directed the conversation. "I can see from looking around that quite a lot of work was done down here. What about the cellar, where's that?"

"Oh the cellar wasn't changed at all my dear. Health and Safety weren't very interested. It was only ever used to store old bits and pieces and it's not used at all nowadays. I don't suppose anyone's been down there for years. There's a trap door down to it somewhere in the storage room next door.

"Ooh!" Josey cried. "Have you ever been down there, Martha? I bet it's terribly dusty and dirty isn't it? Is that where the secret tunnel is? Did you ever see it? Did anyone ever go down there and try to find the treasure?" Josey's words tumbled out in her excitement.

Martha laughed again, "Hold on now, my dear", she spluttered between laughs. "I did go down there once or twice when I was a very young girl as a bit of a dare because it was so dark and musty but I haven't been down there for years and I don't think anyone else has. I seem to recall stories about there once being a tunnel that lead down to the bay. But, that was years ago and the cliff has fallen away in so many places that even if there was a tunnel I doubt that it would be there now and I certainly didn't see sight nor sound of a tunnel when I was down there. Mind you I didn't stay too long it was quite scary and spooky down there full of dust and dirt and cobwebs." She shuddered at the recollection. "Now don't you go getting too excited young lady, you might go and get yourself into trouble. Just you put it out of your head my dear. If there was a tunnel it's long gone and Billy Bones' treasure with it." She laughed again and patted Josey's hand as she saw the glum look replace the excitement on Josey's face. "Now my dears it's been very nice chatting to you but I must clear these tea things away and get myself home before the rain starts again."

"Oh don't worry about clearing away Martha", Kitty said with a smile. "We'll do that for you it won't take a minute and we wouldn't want you to get wet. You'd better go now while there's a break in the weather", she added looking out of the kitchen window to see a little patch of blue sky appearing through the clouds.

"Well that's very kind of you my dears. I'll do just that if you really don't mind. It takes me a little while to get home these days. I'm not quite as nimble as I used to be." Martha smiled as she stood and crossed the room to retrieve her coat and bag. "Perhaps I'll see you again then?" she added hopefully as she walked out of the kitchen.

"Oh yes we'll come and see you again", the children called. "When you're next at work. Thanks Martha. Hope you don't get caught in a shower."

Chapter 9

The three children turned to look at each other. "Well done Josey." Kitty said. "Let's clear these things away quickly and then we'll have a look in the cellar."

Quickly the children stacked the tea things in the sink. Sam washed, Josey wiped and Kitty put away. Within minutes the job was done and they turned their attention to the storage room next door. Sam finished first and wiping his hands he walked through into the next room scanning the floor for the trapdoor Martha had described. The floor was covered in boxes and crates of fresh produce that had been delivered that morning.

"Oh there's load of stuff in here. How are we ever going to find it?" Josey cried coming up behind him.

Sam was still walking around the room pushing aside crates and boxes. Moving to the back of the room, and what Sam guessed was still the outside wall of the old part of the hotel. Sam found a trapdoor under a pile of crates up against the wall. He struggled to push the pile of crates out of the way and puffed over his shoulder to the two girls, "It's here come on give me a hand. I don't know what these crates are full of but they're very heavy."

The two girls rushed over and shoulder to shoulder managed to push the crates aside.

"I think it's potatoes", Josey puffed leaning up against the wall to catch her breath. "I didn't know potatoes could be so heavy."

"Well there are quite a few here Josey", Kitty chuckled putting her hand on Josey's shoulders and doubling over to take a good look at the trapdoor over Sam's shoulder.

Sam was rubbing the dust and dirt away from the trapdoor to reveal a big ring pull at one end and great hinges let into the floor at the other. Sam grabbed the ring pull and heaved. The trapdoor gave a little shudder but didn't move. "I can't lift it. Are you sure all the crates are off it?" Sam said in a somewhat exasperated voice.

"Yes there's nothing on it now Sam", Kitty replied, "But look at the size of it, it must be very heavy."

The trap door was, it must be said, quite large about 30 inches square and the wood looked very thick and tough. Probably oak planking from one of the old ships. It was dark brown and very roughly scored from the centuries of having boxes and crates dragged across it.

"Let's all try pulling together", Josey suggested but when they tried, they found they couldn't all get their hands in the ring pull at the same time.

"Oh how can we do this?" Kitty said in frustration. "What we need is a piece of rope or something that we can put through the ring pull then we can all hold on to it and pull."

"Oh that's a clever idea," Josey said in admiration. "Anyone bring any rope with them?"

"Don't be silly Josey. Why would we have rope with us?" Sam admonished. "It's got to be pretty strong rope to lift something that weight. Let's have a look round to see if there's something in here we can use."

They all moved away from the trapdoor looking between the boxes and crates for a piece of rope or string. Eventually Sam found a box that had plastic straps round it holding it tight shut. "I don't suppose anyone will notice if we make use of these", he said. Calling the girls over Sam pulled one of the straps off the box sideways. Luckily, it was pretty, loose and moved easily. The other strap, for there were two on the box, was much tighter and couldn't be moved no matter how hard he pulled.

"Oh well. I expect we can make do with just one", Sam exclaimed.

The strap he had was about 2 feet long and was formed in a circle. Taking the strap Sam went over to the trap door and passed it through the ring pull. "Right!" he said to his sisters. "You grab hold of that end of the loop and I'll hold this end. When I give the word, we all pull together. Now the trap door will open up against the wall so be careful where you stand."

The two girls stood awkwardly side by side and stooped to hold the strap as firmly as they could while Sam bent down and held the other end.

"One, two, three. Pull!" Sam exclaimed and the three children all pulled together grunting and groaning with the effort. After what seemed an age the trap door started to move and up it came about three or four inches then the strap slipped from Sam's sweaty hands and it crashed back down causing all three children to fall backwards landing on their backsides.

"Oh Sam. What did you do that for?" said Josey picking herself up and rubbing her sore bottom. "That hurt! I shall have a bruise there now", she continued on the point of having a wail.

"Oh come on Jo", said Kitty pulling herself up, "Sam didn't do it on purpose. It's just a very heavy trapdoor. What we need is something to wedge underneath it once we get it up a few inches. That way we can have a rest in between pulls."
"Great idea Kitty", Sam enthused. "There are some logs in this basket in the corner. I tell you what, it's awkward you two pulling together how about if you and I pull Kitty and Josey you put a log under each side when we get it high enough?"

The two girls agreed and Sam and Kitty once more took hold of either end of the strap.

"OK. One, two, three. Pull!" Sam exclaimed and he and Kitty threw themselves back against the strain of the strap and the trap door, having been moved once already, fairly flew out of the floor allowing Josey to push the two logs she held ready in her hands, smartly into the opening.

"Well done. Now let's have a look inside", Kitty said squatting on her haunches and peering through the opening. "No it's no good I can't see a thing. It's very dark down there. Let's get the trapdoor up the rest of the way and see if that's any better."

With one of the children on each of the three moveable sides and now able to get their fingers under the trapdoor it moved quite easily and landed with a faint bump against the storeroom wall.

They all three peered down into the cellar where they could just make out steps leading down. They looked for a light switch on the wall but there wasn't one. In fact, there wasn't even a wall. The steps were attached at the top, to the beams the trapdoor was lying on and seemed to descend into what must have been the middle of the cellar, well away from the walls.

"Oh. There isn't a light switch", Sam said over his shoulder to the two girls. "I guess that the cellar has never been wired up to the electricity. You remember that Martha said they had never done much work down here. Did either of you bring a torch?"

The girls looked at each other "No we didn't Sam. You know we didn't, there wasn't time."

"Well we'd better go and get one now because we're going to need it." Sam turned back to his sisters, "It's pitch black down there. I think we'd all better go back to our rooms and bring back a torch or we're not going to get very far."

"OK Sam", Kitty replied, "But we can't just leave the trapdoor open. Let's close it again and we'll all go and get torches."

"Oh you can get mine Kitty", Josey said with a little smile. "We don't both need to go. I'll stay here on guard."

"No", Kitty said quite firmly. "We'll close it. The kitchen staff will be coming in to prepare the evening meal sometime soon and how would you explain why you're standing next to an open trapdoor if anyone came in here Josey? No, we'll all go upstairs and hope that by the time we get back the staff parlour and storeroom are still empty. Come on now let's go."

Once again using the plastic strap they lowered the trapdoor back in place and Josey turned and trudged after her sister and brother who were scampering away up the stairs. Kitty was right of course but the knowledge of that did nothing to ease Josey's disappointment. She had wanted to stand guard and perhaps venture a little way inside while the others were away. After all, the tunnel and the treasure might just be inside the trapdoor and she was determined to be the one to find it. Still it would be safer if they all went in together. With a little shiver, Josey remembered Sam's words as he retold the story of Cap'n Billy's ghostly visitation. It was easy to forget about that here and now in the light of day but it had looked very black down those cellar steps and she certainly wouldn't like to be down there on her own in the cold and dark when a disembodied hand clutching a cutlass appeared through the wall and threatened her. The very thought of it lent wings to Josey's feet and casting a glance over her shoulder she quickly chased after the other two, grateful for Kitty's intervention.

"Meet you back here", Kitty yelled to Sam as he cut off to go to his own bedroom. The two girls fell into their own room and quickly located their torches. Kitty had a small hand held torch while Josey had a small torch fixed to an elastic headband that she was able to wear on her head so that the torch pointed out from her forehead like a miner's lamp. She used that torch at night when she wanted to read her comic books in bed.

"Don't wear your torch while we're in sight of everyone Josey", Kitty called as Josey was about to leave the bedroom with the torch firmly in place on her head. "Everyone will see it and wonder what we're up to, you silly. Put it in your pocket until we get down to the storeroom."

Josey giggled and pulled the torch off her head and placed it safely in a pocket. "Sorry Kitty I wasn't thinking", she replied. "There's Sam. Hey Sam. Where's your torch?" she called.

"I can't find it", Sam whispered back. "Keep your voice down Jo or we'll have Mum and Dad up here. If you've both got yours that will have to do. I just don't know where mine is. Come on let's go." Sam bounded down the stairs with Kitty and Josey in hot pursuit. They sauntered slowly across the lobby so as not to arouse suspicion and then helter skelter down the stairs to the storeroom once they were safely out of sight.

Sam turned into the staff parlour first motioning the other two to wait while he had a look to see if anyone was there. "It's OK", he whispered over his shoulder. "The kitchen staff haven't come to do the dinner yet." He quickly moved across the staff parlour into the storeroom with the two girls at his heels.

"Alright!" said Kitty once more taking charge and picking up the discarded length of plastic. "Same as before. You and I will pull Sam and you push the logs under Josey."

Up came the trapdoor, quite easily this time so easily in fact that Josey didn't have to place the logs underneath because Kitty and Sam raised the trapdoor fully between them so that it rested quite comfortably against the storeroom wall. Josey had already donned her torch and eagerly she peered over the edge of the trap door and switched her torch on. It lit up a set of steps that descended to the cellar floor, which she could just make out at the end of the torch beam. "Ooh it looks a long way down" she said her courage deserting her at the first.

In the light of her torch beam a cloud of dust swirled and flew upwards caused by the updraft from opening the trapdoor at the same time a low moaning sound whispered around the storeroom. "What's that?" Josey cried falling over backwards as she tried to avoid the dust, which billowed up through the trapdoor.

"It's just dust Josey", Sam spluttered as he tried to clear the dust from his mouth. Unfortunately, Sam had been as eager as Josey and hadn't moved out of the way quite as quickly.

"I know that Sam. I'm talking about the noise. Didn't you hear it, a sort of a moaning noise? I don't like it I'm not going down there", Josey said as she struggled to her feet putting a safe distance between herself and the trap door.

"That's just the wind in the eaves Josey", Kitty replied. "Look the wind's really got up outside." She pointed out of the window in the little storeroom door and the branches of the trees were clearly visible bending this way and that in the strong wind. "I think we might be in for more rain this afternoon so this is a really good time to explore. Come on Jo you've got the best torch you go first that way you can hold on properly with your hands." Kitty took Josey's arm and guided her back to the trapdoor.

Josey looked carefully over the edge, it did look dark down there and the wind was moaning again. She hesitated and then summoning her courage, she sat herself down on the floor and swung her legs over the edge, gingerly reaching out with her feet to find the top step. Suddenly she screamed and leapt up frantically scrabbling at her ankles. "Something touched me, something touched me!" she shouted dancing wildly round and round. Kitty quickly made a dive for the floor and snatched up a fairly, large spider, which she held out in her hand. "Oh Jo it's only a spider", she said holding it out in her hand.

"I don't care. I don't want to go down there. It's a rotten smelly, dusty place and I don't like it", Josey said with tears starting to cloud her eyes.

Kitty shot Sam a warning glance, as he was about to take the mickey out of his younger sister. "It's alright Josey!" she said carrying the spider over to the door and dropping it outside. "It really was only a spider. I tell you what, you give Sam your torch and let him go down first and then you and I can follow."

For a moment, Sam looked aghast. It was all very well laughing at someone else but very different when suddenly he found himself in the front line but he couldn't possibly let his sisters think he might be a bit scared, so summoning his courage and putting on what he thought of as a nonchalant smile Sam said, "Sure I don't mind. Give me your torch Jo and I'll go down first".

Gratefully, Josey handed over her torch and Sam carefully swung his legs over the floor reaching for the first step. He found it and tested its weight with one foot before placing the other foot next to it and putting his whole weight on the ladder. "Seems OK", he murmured looking at his sister's taut expressions. Looking down he shone the torch on to his feet and started to move down the ladder. Kitty knelt down and shone her torch down to the foot of the stair in an attempt to light his way. Coughing and sneezing as he stirred up even more dust Sam made his way down the stair and reaching the bottom without mishap he shone the torch around.

"Well I'm down", he called back to the girls. "Nothing much down here really. Some big old casks lining one side of the cellar and what looks like old broken boxes all over the floor. It's ever so dusty. I shall tie a handkerchief over my nose and mouth. You should do the same before you come down."

"Well isn't there a tunnel entrance?" Josey, once again excited, peered over the edge trying to see in the light of Sam's torch.

"Not that I can see", Sam replied. "You come down next Jo and Kitty and I will light your way. Then Kitty can come down last."

"Good idea Sam", Kitty said. "Come on Jo you go down now and then I'll follow. I don't think we should both go on the ladder at the same time just in case it might break. I guess it's awfully old and might have worm."

"What do you mean worm?" Josey enquired in alarm, dragging her feet away from the opening.

"I only mean woodworm Jo", Kitty replied in exasperation. "Don't be such a wuss. Woodworms just eat wood not people. Now come on or we shall never get down."

With a sulking, little frown and muttering complaints and protests under her breath, Josey swung her legs over the hatch and gingerly made her way down the steps while Sam and Kitty looked on. All of the children now had handkerchiefs tied over their mouths and noses, which muffled their voices. Kitty followed while Sam shone his torch on the steps as she made her way down. Once at the bottom both Kitty and Sam shone their torches around. As Sam had said, old broken boxes and bits of wood littered the floor. Lined up along one very long wall there were five huge casks each bigger than Josey. The other walls were bare and unadorned. Old bricks showed through the plaster here and there and a pile of broken plaster was heaped against the wall, obviously the reason for there being so much dust.

Sam shone his torch at the ceiling and they could see the undersides of the old oak floorboards. No such luxury as a ceiling down here. The children could see cracks of light showing through the storeroom floorboards, which was uncarpeted.

"Well there doesn't seem to be anything around here", Sam said, "and the walls look solid", he continued as he walked across the floor to the nearest wall scattering the broken crates before him.

"Don't do that Sam", Kitty cried. "You're just stirring up the dust again. Walk carefully or we'll all be covered."

Sam reaching the wall struck it gently with the flat of his hand and moved along striking the wall at every pace.

"What are you doing Sam?" Josey questioned, completely lost.

"I'm looking for an entrance to the secret tunnel, silly. There might be a false bit in the wall and if I tap it, it will sound hollow. I saw someone in a film do that once and when they found a hollow bit that's where the secret entrance was."

Sam continued to tap his way around the wall while the girls stood and watched. Eventually Sam came to a stop by the five large casks lined up against the rear wall of the cellar.

"Well, I didn't hear anything that sounded hollow, did you?" he said looking back at his sisters. Both girls shook their heads and walked towards him Kitty's torch bobbing across the floor as she walked. Josey tried to keep up with her not wanting to be left alone without a light she stumbled tripping on one of the old broken crates that littered the floor. Poor Josey tangled in the crate and fell down with thump.

"Oh Kitty! Remember that I'm here too I can't see anything without a torch. You could at least have shone your torch so I could see too!" Josey was cross and scared. She pulled her foot from the broken crate, and in temper picked the crate up and flung it from her across the cellar where it smacked into one of the five giant casks that lined the wall. Picking herself up Josey dusted herself down as best she could, brushing dust and cobwebs from her clothes asking Kitty to shine her torch so she could see what she was doing.

"Did you hear that you two?" Sam called interrupting the girls bickering.

"Hear what?" Josey said in temper. "Oh Kitty do keep that torch still please. I can't see what I'm doing."

"The cask you hit with that wood sounded hollow", Sam answered.

"Well I don't suppose any of them are still full of whatever it was they had in them", Josey replied sulkily while trying to make sure that there were no lingering cobwebs adorning her legs. "They're bound to be empty aren't they?"

"Yes but hold on a minute", Sam muttered. "One of these casks might conceal the entrance to the tunnel".

Sam went to the first of the casks and started tapping. "That's empty." On to the second. "That's empty too" and so on down the line. All the casks sounded empty. Sam went back down the line this time with girls by his side. Starting from the right hand end of the line, they went along tapping and pressing the front of each cask. They were trying to see if there was some sort of secret door let into the front of any of the casks. Once again down the line they went, nothing had moved and they couldn't see in the light of their torches that there was any sort of door or opening anywhere. They stood in front of the last cask in the line and looked back at the others. In the front of each cask, low down probably no more than three inches from the bottom was a tap sort of thing.

"What are those?" Josey said pointing down.

"That's what's called a spigot", Kitty said grandly. "It's the tap for the cask. If you turn it the liquid inside runs through the spigot and out at the bottom."

"Ooh! Let's have a go", Josey said quite excited and forgetting her previous sulk. "Shine your light on this one", she said bending down and grabbing hold of the nearest spigot. Exerting all her strength, she turned the tap but nothing happened.

"Well, nothing in there then", said Sam moving on to the next one.

"Oh Sam do let me do it", Josey said pushing him out of the way. "You two have got the torches I can use both hands" So saying she bent down to spigot number two and turned. Once again nothing. Quickly moving on Josey grasped the third spigot, which was on the middle cask and turned. To her surprise and the consternation of the others, the spigot turned easily and as it turned the whole front of the cask swivelled on hinges, which were concealed top and bottom of the cask so that half the front pushed out and half pushed in. Josey stumbled into Sam just managing to avoid being knocked down, by the speed with which the secret door opened.

"Blimey!" muttered Sam as they all stood in opened mouthed amazement staring into the dark inner of the cask. "It's a false front. This must be the entrance to the tunnel. We've found it!" Sam turned to the two girls his face shining with delight. Brandishing his cutlass and with Josey's torch still attached firmly to his head, Sam made to move forwards into the cask.

As Sam moved forward, a sudden noise filled the old cask and a hushed wind blew steadily through the opening. Filling the air with a sighing moan and blowing strings of cobweb from inside the cask into their faces. The children stopped and listened. The moaning sigh gradually faded away and the cobwebs fluttered back into their places inside the cask.

Josey took a step backwards and said, "I don't like this! That didn't sound very nice. What do you think it can be? It might be Cap'n Billy's ghost come to get us. He's bound to be protecting his treasure still isn't he or else why would he have appeared to you last night Sam?"

"It's OK Jo", Sam said standing forward in front of the girls, cutlass in hand. "It's just the wind. I don't suppose this door has been opened for ages and ages. It's only natural for the wind to blow up through it. That's what made the noise, don't you think so Kitty?"

As Sam turned towards Kitty for support a final gust of wind, stronger than before blew sharply through the opening. The cobwebs blew out like streamers slapping their hands and faces. Suddenly, the children heard a massive crash behind them, the echoes bouncing off the old cellar walls causing dust to stir from the floor and spread through the air like a fine mist. The children jumped and whirled round shining the torches before them.

"Oh No!" Sam shouted. "The trapdoor in the storeroom. It's closed!"

Quickly Sam ran towards the ladder and dropping the cutlass on the floor quickly climbed to the top and heaved against the trapdoor with his hands and shoulders trying desperately to lift it. Struggling and panting Sam strained while the girls yelled their encouragement.

"It's no good I can't shift it", Sam called. "I can't shift it!"

The note of desperation in his voice unnerved the girls and Josey clutched at Kitty's arm. "Oh Kitty what are we going to do?"

Kitty bit back her tears and said, "Let me try to get up there with you Sam. We might be able to lift it if we push together." Pushing her torch into Josey's trembling fingers she started up the ladder but it soon became obvious that no matter how they tried they couldn't stand on the ladder side by side and get sufficient purchase to push with both hands. Mainly, because they had to use one hand to hang on to the ladder to stop them from falling off.

"It's no use", Kitty finally said. "We can't do it. We'll have to think of something else."

"I know", Josey called. "Let's shout as loud as we can. Someone's bound to hear us after all the kitchen staff will probably be back by now."

"Good idea Jo", Sam said. "OK. One, two three" and on the count of three the children all yelled and called until their throats hurt with the strain.

"Listen", said Kitty. "Listen", but there was no answering reply, no comforting sound of feet overhead. They were alone in the dark.

Chapter 10

Kitty and Sam dropped the last few feet to the ground and Kitty found Josey's hand to give her a squeeze. "We must be brave now", Kitty said. "It's OK. We've got our torches and someone is bound to come looking for us, we're not in any danger, not really." Kitty gave Josey another squeeze and the three children looked at each other in the torchlight.

"Well what do we do now?" Josey said in a very small voice but being incredibly brave and blinking back the tears that were filling her eyes.

Sam drew himself up, swished his cutlass in the air. "As I see it we can either stay here and yell some more until someone hears us and lifts the trapdoor or we can explore a bit by going into the tunnel. After all that is why we came down here in the first place don't forget. We came to find the treasure."

"What about that groaning noise?" Josey whispered. "You don't think it's really Cap'n Billy's ghost do you?"

Kitty and Sam stole a glance at each other knowing that whatever they really felt they must not let Josey see they were worried or she would howl and wail and they'd never get her to do anything. Together they said, "Oh no! Josey that was just the wind. That's what blew the trapdoor closed."

"You remember Josey when we're at home and we open the front door when the back door is already open the wind blows through and the back door slams. It happens all the time doesn't it?" Kitty tried to sound confident and reassuring.

"Yes", Josey replied a little hesitantly, "But we're not in the dark at home and there aren't any ghosts there." Josey gripped Kitty's hand harder and moved closer to Sam so that they stood in a little knot together at the bottom of the stairs.

"Well, we've got to do something we can't just stand here for the rest of the day. I'm for going forward. You never know we might find the treasure but we might also find a way out of here. Come on!" Sam stepped away from the girls and moved towards the old cask that concealed what they hoped was the tunnel, the treasure and an exit.

Sam shone his torch forward and walked across the floor guiding the torch beam into the opening. He flashed it around inside and could see that apart from a blanket of cobwebs clinging to the sides of the cask there was no back to it. He judged that he and the girls could easily squeeze inside and that their heads wouldn't even come near the top of the cask.

"This must have been quite a squeeze for Cap'n Billy and his crew", he said stepping forward into the opening. "Come on you two let's go. I'll go first, Josey next and Kitty you bring up the rear."

Josey, cringing from the nasty cobwebs and the thought of lurking spiders, slipped inside the cask pressing herself away from the sides. Kitty shining her torch over Josey's shoulder came immediately behind. The three children shuffled their way forwards through the cask and out of the back. Once through the cask they felt a little better, a slight breeze moved around them and the air felt fresher and cleaner.

The tunnel was not all that big, just wide enough for the children to move down it three abreast. Sam and Kitty stood either side of Josey and could feel the walls of the tunnel with their outstretched hands. Sam reached up above his head with the cutlass and touched the ceiling of the tunnel not far above his head. Gingerly they moved forward. The floor was reasonably smooth and level except where bits of the wall or ceiling had fallen away and at those places they had to be quite careful so as not to stumble and fall on the broken ground. Everywhere was quite dry and dusty. As they walked along the sound of their footfalls echoed back through tunnel and occasionally, they stopped, listening to see if they could hear anything else but caught only the sound of their own breathing and the beating of their hearts.

At first the tunnel was quite level but then after a short while it began to slope downwards, gently at first and then quite sharply so they had to be even more careful as they made their way along. Josey seemed to be having most difficulty as she had the shortest legs and made the job harder for herself by refusing to release Kitty and Sam's hands, which she clung to with a quiet, desperate strength. A few times, she almost fell but was held up by her brother and sister.

After a little while of stumbling along in relative silence Sam suddenly gave a fearful low moaning groan.

"What is it Sam?" Josey clutched him even more fiercely. "What's wrong? What's the matter?"

Sam giggled, "Oh that got you didn't it Jo? Did you think Cap'n Billy had come to call?"

Josey immediately released his hand and punched his arm. "Oh Sam you're so wicked. You frightened the life out of me." Releasing Kitty's hand she gave him another hard push sending him crashing into the side of the tunnel.

"Oh steady on Josey. I was only having a bit of a laugh", Sam pushed himself upright and taking the torch from his head, he held it under his chin and gave another low moan pulling a hideous face in the shadows cast by the torchlight.

"Oh that doesn't scare me", Josey retorted. "You look like that all the time".

Kitty started to laugh as did Sam then they all started to make ghostly noises, even Josey.

"That's better. It's only darkness, there are no ghosts down here", Sam smiled, his teeth flashing in the darkness. "Come on let's move on. We're going downhill quite sharply so we must be following the contours of the cliff down to the sea. It won't be long before we reach the bottom I reckon, and then we'll be able to find our way out."

The children moved forward again the torches shining across the tunnel floor. After a few paces, they all felt a change in the breeze that was gently blowing in their faces. The breeze dropped and then gusted sharply and the low groaning moan echoed eerily around them bringing a chill and goose bumps that started out on their bare arms.

"Oh stop it Sam!" Josey cried, more in hope than anger.

"It wasn't me that time. I promise", Sam had stopped and turned shining his torch back the way they had come. "Which way did it come from I couldn't tell? It must just have been the wind again I felt it change didn't you?"

The two girls nodded their heads and once more holding hands they crept on down the passage heading downward as before. After a little while, the tunnel took a fairly sharp turn to the left where the walls fell away and it opened out to become quite wide. Kitty and Sam could no longer touch the sides of the tunnel.

Flashing their torches around, they made out that the tunnel had opened into a sort of cavern. The tunnel came in at one side and continued on at the other. In one wall a series of deep shelves had been cut into the rock face and a jumble of things still lay upon them. Quickly walking over the children started to explore the shelves all thoughts of groaning ghosts lost in their excitement. Jostling each other to be first to lay hands on the bits of jumble they searched the shelves eagerly anticipating the clink of golden coins and jewels. Instead, they found an odd assortment of stuff. A bundle of large candles, a flint and some tinder in a little tin box, several empty bottles, a pair of leather gloves, some dirty old sacking, a knife and an old flintlock pistol both of which were very rusty.

"No treasure. How disappointing. I thought we'd found it", as he said that Sam's torch began to flicker and dim. "Oh no! The battery is beginning to fail. We don't want to be left in the dark. Switch your torch off Kitty then when this one fails we'll have yours at least".

"But what happens when Kitty's torch runs out?" a frightened Josey voiced the thought that was in each of their minds.

"Wait a bit", Kitty suddenly exclaimed scrabbling in the pile of junk on the shelves. "There are candles here. We can light them".

"How? We don't have any matches, do we?" Josey asked hopefully.

Kitty thrust the candles at Josey and scrabbled some more in the jumble, "No but I did see a tinder box in here somewhere. If we could get that to work then we could light the candles."

Josey didn't know what a tinderbox was but she helped search for it anyway. Kitty pulled a little tin box from the pile of jumble and held it out triumphantly, "Here it is look."

By the light of Sam's torch Kitty opened the little box to reveal a flint and a striker nestling in some close packed wadding, which looked something like cotton wool. Quickly Kitty teased the wadding out so that it was loose.

"It still looks dry so this might work", Kitty said as she balanced the box on the rock shelf. Taking the flint and striker in her hands, she proceeded to strike the flint against the striker, a small thin roughly grooved metal strip. As she did so, a series of small sparks flew from the end of the flint. Kitty leaned over the tinderbox and the wadding and struck the flint directly over the wadding. Sparks fell onto the wadding and briefly smouldered then went out.

"Sam shine your torch on the box. Josey when the sparks hit the tinder you blow very gently and try to fan the spark into a flame", Kitty commanded anxiously as the light of Sam's torch became dimmer by the second.

Josey leaned down with her face quite close to the box, Sam shone the torch directly over her shoulder and Kitty struck the flint again and again so that the sparks hit the tinder. Josey gently breathed on the sparks as they hit the tinder. One or two of them started to smoulder and smoke spiralled up. Josey blew a little harder as Kitty then pulled at the wadding dropping little bits over the top of the smouldering sparks. Quite suddenly as if it had a life of its own a small flame licked up through the tinder and Kitty grabbing one of the candles quickly placed the wick in the flame where it soon caught and its light fought the all consuming darkness forcing it to retreat. The children stood there in a small pool of light with the darkness flickering around them.

Kitty closed the tinderbox saying, "We must save the tinder in case we need it later. Here Josey hold this candle while I get another. Sam you can switch your torch off now it's better to save it now we've got the candles", she withdrew another candle from the bundle and lit it from the flame of the first.

"What luck we found the candles", Sam exclaimed. "Wherever did you learn about tinder boxes Kitty? I wouldn't have known what to do."

"Oh I saw it in an old film on TV", Kitty replied. "That's how they made fire before they invented matches. We were awfully, lucky to find candles and a tinderbox weren't we? And so lucky they were dry".

Josey passed her candle to Sam and put her arms around Kitty giving her a big hug. "Oh I have such a clever sister", she said giving Kitty the biggest squeeze of her life.

"Well let's have a candle each", Kitty went on, pulling another candle from the bundle. "That way we don't have to worry about lighting the way. We've got at least a dozen here and they're all quite big." She then lit another candle and presented it to Josey.

With all three children holding up a large candle each the light was indeed quite bright, bright enough for them to see that the cavern they were in was quite large with a high roof.

"OK now we've got light let's have a good look around", Sam suggested. "This might be the place Cap'n Billy secreted his treasure. Come on start looking you two."

The girls busied themselves making sure they hadn't missed anything on the shelves while Sam wandered off to a dark corner by the end of the hewn out shelves. Moving into the darkest shadows Sam stumbled over something lying on the floor. Leaning down and holding his candle so that the light spilled down to his feet Sam looked down in horror as he realised that he had stumbled into a pile of bones and that pile of bones was wearing trousers.

Sam leapt back in horror. "Kitty, Josey come here quick", recovering a little Sam stepped gingerly back towards his gruesome find. Holding his candle high he called over his shoulder, "I've found a skeleton."

The girls hurried up and with the three candles held high, they could see that Sam was right. A skeleton with scraps of tattered clothing still clinging to the legs and torso lay with its back propped against the wall, legs lying across the floor. A rusty cutlass was still visible pushed through the rib bones high up on its left side. Beside it, another skeleton lay on its side in a crumpled heap. Once again, scraps of clothing still clung to the frame and a battered hat lay next to its head.

"Well it's easy to see what happened here", Sam said with the authority of someone who had read and played pirates throughout that summer. "He was stabbed through the heart and he", indicating the other skeleton, "was bashed on the head. Cap'n Billy's crew no doubt. I bet he 'did them in' after they'd lugged his treasure down here for him."

"Oh how awful", Josey cried, "Why would he do that when they must have been his friends?"

"So that they couldn't give away the secret of where his treasure was buried, silly. That's what pirates did and Cap'n Billy probably went to his grave without spending so much as a penny of it. Too worried that someone would see him coming and going. What a waste. Now, all we have to do is find where he put it then we can carry it out of here and live like millionaires. Won't Mum and Dad be surprised?"

Chapter 11

The children stood there, a strange sight in the dark cavern. Three children all holding candles aloft while at their feet lay the bones of long dead men who had been stabbed and bludgeoned to death to preserve the secret of Cap'n Billy Bones' treasure.

Josey found it hard to lift her eyes from the gruesome sight. Something about the vacant eye sockets in the skull and the cutlass still lodged in the chest of the skeleton, held a fascination for her. She didn't want to look but couldn't help herself it was just so awful. She couldn't help thinking about how these two poor men had come to their end. Killed and left to rot down here in the darkness. "He must have been very wicked", she said.

"Who?" Kitty enquired.

"Cap'n Billy Bones. I mean he brought these two men down here and then killed them in cold blood. I'm glad he didn't live to spend his treasure he didn't deserve it."

This was the closest any of the children had been to death, apart from pet guinea pigs and birds at home. For Josey this was an awful sight but for Kitty and Sam, the excitement of perhaps finding the treasure enabled them to forget that these skeletons were once men. They had already begun to move away from Josey and make a search of the shadows and crevices looking for a treasure chest or a bag or sack. Something, anything that looked like it could contain gold and jewels.

While Josey stood there uncertain of her feelings and not sure of quite what to do next the flame of the candle in her hand flickered, a sudden chilly draft of wind wrapped her in its icy hand and the same low groaning moan filled the cavern.

Josey dropped her candle in shock and surprise and called out in some ungovernable, unfathomable, primeval cry of fear, throwing her head back and looking up to the ceiling as if calling on God to come to her aid. As she looked up her eyes wide in horror, she saw a light, a faint glow against the blackness of the cavern's roof. She pointed upwards gasping, "Look, look! What's that?" as Kitty and Sam rushed back to her side.

Sam threw his arm around her, "It's OK Josey. It's OK", while Kitty scrabbled on the floor for Josey's candle that had blown out in the fall to the ground.

Sam's eyes followed Josey's outstretched arm and shielding his own candle's flame he made out the glow, the glimmer of light that Josey had seen.

"It's OK Josey", he repeated as Kitty placed the relit candle in Josey's hand. "I don't know what that is or where the noise came from but we're here there's nothing to be afraid of. Look Kitty, up there. Cover your candle's flame and look up. Can you see it?"

"Yes", Kitty gasped. "What is it? Where's it coming from?"

Together, gripping each other tightly they shuffled forward moving towards the light that was showing high above their heads. They reached the end of the cleft where the skeletons lay and found that it didn't end as they had thought but it turned a corner and there in front of them lay a sort of chimney to the sky. High above them up a natural fissure in the rock they could see the sky. The light was the sun burning high above them and above the cliff top.

The chimney, for that's how they thought of it, started in the roof of the cavern and led almost directly upwards through the rock to the top of the cliff. The roof was about three metres high, too far for them to reach but what a relief to be standing there in the dark and to see the sun. They clutched each other and yelled. "The sun, the sun. Is anyone up there? Can you hear us? Help! Help! Help!" There was no reply.

After a while, they stopped shouting and Josey, now recovered from her fright, wiped the tears from her cheeks and said, "I wonder if we can get out this way?"

She was merely voicing the thoughts of Kitty and Sam. Sam moved over to the side of the cavern and looked at the wall for footholds but there were none and anyway the chimney was directly overhead away from the walls. They would never be able to climb up to it.

"Here Josey. Climb on my shoulders and see if you can reach up to the chimney."
Josey tried with Kitty helping her up onto Sam's shoulders but even standing at her full height there was no way she was going to be able to reach up high enough to pull herself up the chimney. She climbed down and the dispirited children sat on the floor in the sunlight which was filtering down.

A sudden gust of wind blew directly down the chimney causing their candle flames to flicker and bringing with it the deep, groaning moan that had so unnerved them before. Josey clutched at Sam with her free hand but Sam stood up and said, "That's it! That's what's causing the moan. It's not Cap'n Billy it's this chimney, it's acting like a sort of whistle. Like, oh you know, when you blow over the top of a bottle and it makes sound like a foghorn. That's what's happening with this chimney. It's not a ghost. It's a big rock bottle". Sam turned to the others grinning and laughing, "Fancy us all being scared of a rock bottle", as he said that another gust of wind hit the chimney and a short low moan reverberated through the cavern as it had before. This time Josey laughed and Kitty sounded an imaginary foghorn, dropping her voice low and competing with the wind.

As they laughed, the fear left them and they became themselves once more. Kitty looked around her and said, "Well now that Cap'n Billy's ghost has been laid to rest it seems to me that the skeletons we found are a pretty sure indication that the treasure must be here somewhere or else Cap'n Billy wouldn't have killed them would he?" she looked enquiringly at the others. "But where, that's the question. Now Sam just read us that rhyme again it might contain a clue we've overlooked."

Sam pulled the small folded paper from his pocket and began to recite.

Billy Bones will have his say
That Treasure is where ye find it
Where dead men's eyes stare up and pray
Beneath the rocks ye'll find it

Now ye've got the treasure map
T'is in ye'r hands this day

There may be more than one mishap
Afore you end the play

The tunnel's hidden. Ye must take care
My treasure it be waiting
Down in the depths, beware, beware
Straight down below with Satan

Look to the window up on high
Ye see the gleaming gold
It's there ye see, tho' times gone by
Ye have to, must be bold

Now I will come and spike your gun
I must be here it seems
Until the treasure it be gone
To feed some poor man's dreams

For this I tell ye mortal fool
I hid it good, and well
The bones of my old faithful crew
Still guard it now, farewell

"No clues there, other than the bit about the tunnel", Sam scratched his head. "Let's have a good look around just here. Look in all the corners perhaps we've missed something."

The two girls moved away and started searching in the darker recesses of the cleft neither one wanting to move back and search near the skeletons. Sam pulled the map from his pocket and peered at it again in the light from his candle. No nothing new there that he could see. He folded the map and stowed it away in his pocket. A gust of wind moaned down the chimney and Sam looked up at the sky above. As he did so a cloud rolled across the opening at the top and full sunlight shone its rays directly down the chimney into Sam's upturned face. A flash of light appeared half way to the top. Sam rubbed his eyes and looked again. Yes, there it was half way up on the left hand side.

"Kitty, Josey. Come here quick look, look", Sam pointed towards the flash and both girls tumbled breathlessly to his side in time to see the sunlight glinting off the left hand wall of the chimney.

"What's that?" Kitty peered upwards trying to get a better look. "It must be metal or maybe glass to reflect the sunlight like that."

"Do you think it could be the treasure?" Josey jumped up and down, "Oh it must be. It must be."

Sam suddenly gasped and took out the rhyme from his pocket. Unfolding it he said, "Yes, of course, how could I be so silly? Look here at the fourth verse."

Look to the window up on high
Ye see the gleaming gold
It's there ye see, tho' times gone by
Ye have to, must be bold

"I never really understood that. I thought it was something to do with Cap'n Billy coming to me in the middle of the night with his hand coming through my window but now I see it's not talking about my bedroom window, it's talking about the chimney and the window to the sky. See, the opening at the top of the chimney is just like an attic window."

Look to the window up on high
Ye see the gleaming gold

"We've found it! We've found it! It must be the treasure!" All three children looked at each other in open-mouthed amazement. "But how do we reach it?" Josey looked crestfallen, "It's too high!"

Sam picked up a stone from the floor and threw it upwards aiming towards the flash of sunlight but stone simply bounced of the rock wall and fell back narrowly missing Kitty.

"Oi! Do be careful Sam", Kitty yelled jumping out of the way of the falling stone. "Anyway we don't know that it is the treasure. Look up there now, I can't see anything shining, it was probably just a trick of the light. The sun glinting off a bit of shiny rock. What we've got to do is get out of here."

The smiles vanished from Sam and Josey's faces at Kitty's words. Get out of here! Yes but how?

The sound of Josey's tummy rumbling made them all realise that the time had been wearing away and it was almost late afternoon.

"We've missed tea", the ever-practical Kitty went on "So Mum and Dad will have missed us and must be searching already. We've got three choices. We can stay here and shout and hope some passer by hears us. We can go back up the tunnel to the cellar and shout there for help and hope the kitchen staff might hear us or we can go on down the tunnel and see if we can get out to the beach." She looked enquiringly at the others.

"Well I don't know", Josey said, "What do you think we should do Kitty?"

Sam shrugged his shoulders in agreement with Josey. Kitty was the practical one she would make the best choice.

"Well", Kitty considered, "I don't think there's much chance of someone happening along this little bit of cliff do you? Everyone will stick to the path so there's not much chance of them hearing our calls. Going back to the cellar doesn't seem to be any good either. We know we can't lift the trapdoor and the cellar walls and ceiling are so thick that there's not much chance of being heard there either."

"But Mum and Dad may have talked to old Martha", Josey interrupted, "She would have told them we were interested in the cellar."

"Yes but she's gone home don't forget. At this moment in time, no one knows we're stuck down here. I think the only thing to do is go on down the tunnel and see if we can get out to the beach."

"I think you're right Kitty", Sam had been thinking it through as well. "The tunnel must have come out on the beach when it was first dug. The map shows it does, so it's has to be worth a go. It's better than standing around waiting anyway." Turning away Sam strode out of the cleft and made towards the tunnel mouth, which they hoped led down to the beach.

Skirting the skeletons Kitty and Josey followed. Kitty scooped up the remaining candles as she went past the rock shelf. "Just in case we need them", she said in an aside to Josey and the two of them, candles held high followed Sam down the tunnel and, they hoped, to the beach.

Chapter 12

The two girls joined Sam in the tunnel entrance and as before, they walked together side by side, candles held aloft lighting their way. After a few short paces, the tunnel walls pressed in either side of them so that they had to walk shoulder to shoulder almost jostling each other in their attempt to remain together. Suddenly Josey cried out as the hot wax from the candle trickled down on to her hand. She dropped the candle and yelled, "Ouch that's hot!"

"Press your hand against the tunnel wall", Kitty instructed, "That's cold and wet. It'll take the heat out." Josey did as she was told and the cooling tunnel wall gave relief to the minor burn. "Pull your sleeve over your hand. That way the hot wax won't get on your skin", Kitty said as she retrieved Josey's dropped candle. "You just hold our hands instead Josey there's really no need for us all to have a candle." She gave Josey's hand a little rub. "There's no damage done. See the wax peels off and your skin is OK." Kitty tucked Josey's candle into her pocket with the others, took Josey's hand and signing to Sam moved on cautiously down the tunnel.

As they walked on it became obvious that here the tunnel had fared far worse than the upper part. At these lower levels, it dropped away quite steeply now and the floor was littered with piles of rubble where a wall or ceiling had crumbled. It made it quite difficult to walk abreast and eventually the three children were forced to walk in single file. The smell of the sea was all pervasive and damp chilled the air. The children shivered in the cold and became quite afraid.

"Do you think we should go on?" Josey whispered. For down here it was unthinkable to talk in normal tones, the very air seemed still and the walls appeared to lean in listening to their laboured breathing.

Sam stopped and held his candle high moving it around lighting up the tunnel. "I'm not sure but I think we must be getting quite close to beach level. Let's go on a little further it would be a shame to come all this way and turn back without knowing whether there's a way out down here or not."

Nodding her agreement Kitty gave Josey an encouraging squeeze, "Just a little further Josey. The way out may be only just around the corner." Holding Josey's hand, she moved forward and together the three children stumbled over the next pile of rubble and round a bend before feeling a faint draft blowing in their faces and then the sound of the sea, which became clearer and clearer as they moved forwards. Now the walls and floor became really damp, with pools of water occasionally under their feet on the tunnel floor and water marks on the walls starting low down but moving higher and higher the further they went down. Rounding yet another bend, the children suddenly heard the sea very clearly as it echoed up the tunnel and they felt water soaking their feet.

"There's water on the floor", Josey called. "We must have reached the sea. There's no way out here."

Holding their candles high the children saw that Josey was right. They could see the water just a little way ahead. The waves moved with the regular rhythm ebbing and flowing, moving inexorably towards them.

"The tide must have turned", Sam said disappointment drenching his words. "Josey's right Kitty, there's no way out for us here."

As they stood and watched, the sea moved up the tunnel with surprising speed.
"I think we'd better get out of here quickly", Sam went on. "That water is moving pretty fast, if we don't hurry we're going to get awfully wet." As he said that, the water gave an extra spurt and small waves licked at their feet.

The children turned and quickly began to retrace their steps back up the tunnel. They hadn't realised quite how steeply the tunnel had dropped down. Only now as they were forced to climb to flee the oncoming tide did they recognise quite how much effort they needed to go back the way they'd come.

Now the wreckage of the collapsing walls proved to be a real hindrance. Stumbling and falling, bruising their shins and knees, sometimes forced to use their hands to get past a particularly nasty pile of rubble they breathlessly pushed on upwards while the sea rushed to catch them.

The candles now were almost stumps in Kitty and Sam's hands. The light flickered and wavered as they pushed, jostled and stumbled up the slope. The sound of the sea was now very loud as the incoming tide pushed its way forward into the tunnel and more than once the children felt the spray as a big wave broke against the tunnel wall.

Chests heaving the children stopped as Kitty called a halt.

"I can't hold this stump of a candle any more", she panted, "Hold on while I light another."

"Get one for me Kitty", Sam said as he juggled the remaining stump of his candle from one hand to the other trying to avoid the hot, liquid wax that was now streaming down the inch long stump.

Kitty gave Josey two candles and she lit both from Kitty's candle. Handing one to Kitty and one to Sam she said, "Come on then let's go quickly. I can hear the sea catching up."

The children heard the rush and whoosh of the waves before they turned and saw the tide running quickly up the incline behind them.

"OK", Sam said pushing on quickly in the lead with Kitty and Josey stumbling along behind him. More than once Josey fell and with Sam reaching behind him to pull her up and Kitty pushing her along from behind they outpaced the inrushing tide and finally found themselves back in the cavern bumped and bruised, panting for breath. They lay on the floor recovering themselves.

"Well that was a bit scary", Sam said with the studied nonchalance of a film star hero. "But we'll be alright here. The floor and walls are really dry here. I don't think the tide ever gets up this far."

Josey sat up, "But we're back here now. How on earth are we going to get out? Don't forget we thought the beach was our best hope!" She looked from one to the other searching their faces. Both her siblings looked back at her blankly. They had run out of ideas.

"I don't know Josey", Sam said after a long pause, "I guess we'll just have to go back to the cellar and yell. As we said before someone must be looking for us by now. We'll just have to hope they hear us." Sam looked to Kitty for confirmation.

Kitty nodded her head, "I think you're right Sam. We certainly can't get out by the beach we've proven that and we know we can't climb up the chimney." She said nodding towards the cleft in the rock that housed the skeletons and Cap'n Billy's 'window'.

The children dragged themselves to their feet and Josey said, "Let's just have one more shout underneath the chimney. You never know someone might be passing."

"Ok Jo. I suppose it's worth another shout", Sam replied and they all made their way past the skeletons to stand under the chimney looking up to the patch of blue sky they could see tantalizingly close overhead.

They stood underneath and called as loudly as they could. The echo of their voices rocked around the cavern and up the chimney but no answering shout came. Josey's eyes were filling with tears. "I wish Daddy was here. I wish we'd never found the rotten old treasure map. I wish we'd never found the rotten cellar and the rotten tunnel."

Kitty put a comforting arm around her and as she did so, the candle in Kitty's hand came in front of Josey's face. She noticed that the candle gave off quite a thick black smoke that spiralled upwards disappearing up the chimney. She shrugged off Kitty's arm and said, "Smoke!"

Kitty and Sam looked at her in alarm, "What do you mean?"

"Smoke", Josey repeated. "Look, look! The smoke from the candle goes up the chimney." The other two looked at her blankly. "If we could start a fire down here and make lots of smoke, the smoke would go up the chimney and somebody would see it", she finished excitedly.

Sam was the first to recover and see the possibility. "You're right Jo", he said, "Well done. Let's see what we can find that we can make a fire from. Come on Kitty. We need something that will burn and then something that will make lots of smoke", he pressed back into the cavern already beginning to search. The girls joined him.

Kitty found the old sacking. Sam found the old lantern and looked to see if there was any lamp oil still in it. There wasn't but he pulled the wick from it anyway.

Josey picked her way around the skeletons and found a couple of small broken casks, which smelled as though they might once have been filled with strong rum or brandy. "Here you two", she called, "I've found some old casks."

Between them, the children pulled the casks out of the shadows and placed them under the chimney. Sam took out his cutlass saying, "We need to break these up a bit first. I'll see what I can do with this."

Kitty and Josey bravely went back to the skeletons and Kitty pulled the old cutlass from between the rib bones of the first skeleton they had discovered. Both girls shuddered as the metal blade rasped against the old cracked bones.

"Come on", Kitty said, and lead the way back to where Sam was busily chopping one of the casks into small fragments. Kitty immediately attacked the other cask and while the cutlasses weren't exactly axes they managed to break and splinter the wood into reasonably small fragments while Josey held a candle in each hand to give them enough light to work by.

Sam cut a piece of the sacking and placed it on the ground directly under the chimney. On top of this, he placed a small pile of chippings from the broken casks. Taking both candles from Josey, he dripped hot wax over the wood chippings and the sacking then he placed one of the candles in the centre of the woodpile and sat back on his haunches. The candle continued to burn and the sacking, which was covered in candle wax, also began to smoulder and then burn. The splinters of wood caught and soon small flames licked around the whole fire.

Kitty was prepared with more wood and she placed this gently on top of the flames careful not to smother the fire and careful not to burn herself in the process. Within minutes, the fire was burning prettily. They stood back and admired the small bonfire with satisfaction until suddenly Kitty said, "There's no smoke! It's a great fire but there's no smoke! Everything is as dry as old bones. We need something damp."

They looked at each other downcast. "There's plenty of water back down the tunnel", Josey said hopefully.

"We're none of us going back down there", Kitty said firmly.

"Well, we'll just have to make the sacks wet ourselves", Sam said with a grin.

"How?" Josey enquired looking confused. "We don't have any water, do we?"

Without saying a word Sam picked up a sack, gave Kitty a meaningful look and walked out of the cleft back into the cavern. As Josey began to follow Sam, Kitty tugged at her arm.

"No Josey don't", she said pulling Josey back. "Sam's gone to make some water." Faintly, they both heard the patter of water splashing onto the sacking.

"Oh", Josey giggled. "I understand."

Sam walked back into the cleft and holding a sack by its corner. The sack was decidedly damp in the middle. "Better put on a bit more wood Kitty", Sam said. "We don't want to smother the flame."

Kitty placed some more wood on the fire and it burned and crackled happily. The old wood had been soaked in rum and brandy for years and now it burned with a bright light. Gingerly, Sam placed the sacking over the top of the flames and immediately smoke billowed up filling the chimney within seconds. The children stood back from the fire and Kitty said, "Now call as loudly as you can. It's our only hope!"

Chapter 13

With the thick smoke spiralling up the chimney, the children stood back and filling their lungs called as loudly as they could. The remaining sacks were placed on top of the wet one and even more smoke issued forth, the flames almost completely quenched. Thick grey, black smoke billowed around them and up the chimney.

The children called and called until their throats ached. The smoke was rolling all around them in the cavern as it crept out from under the sacking that Sam had thrown on top of the fire. Just as they had begun to despair, with eyes streaming and lungs and throats burning, their uplifted faces saw a shadow pass over the sky window at the top of the chimney. A familiar voice called down to them.

"Is that you? Good God! What on earth are you doing down there. Are you hurt?"

It was Dad! The children felt dizzy with relief.

"Sam, whatever it is that's making all this smoke, pull it off the fire. I can't see a thing."

Sam and Kitty quickly pulled the sacking from the fire and the children stamped on it until the flames were gone.

"Where on earth have you been? We've been searching for hours. How on earth did you get down there?" Dad's anxious face was now visible against the backdrop of the late afternoon sky.

The children all shouted back at once.

"We were searching for treasure." Josey called.

"We couldn't get back out again," Kitty explained.

"We've found some skeletons," Sam grinned in excitement.

"Whoa! One at a time. One at a time. Now, Kitty how did you get down there? Did you fall?" Dad was worried.

"No we came through the storeroom cellar from the hotel but the trapdoor fell shut and we couldn't get it open and no one heard us calling so we had to follow the tunnel down here", Kitty replied trying to keep calm and trying to stop Josey jumping up and down.

"We found a map Dad. A treasure map", Sam couldn't contain his excitement either. "It was in the old attic in the hotel and…"

"Hold on Sam. You can all tell me the whole story once I get you out of there. Now I guess you can't reach up and climb or you would have done that by now. It doesn't look too far down. How high from the floor does this chimney start Kitty?"

"About three metres," Kitty replied judging the distance with her eye.

"Not too bad then. What about this trapdoor in the storeroom that fell shut, do you think I'd be able to lift it from this side?" Dad said considering his options.

"Oh yes," Sam immediately responded. "I did try, well Kitty and I tried together and it did move a bit but we weren't quite strong enough."

"Right put that fire out and move out of the way."

The children's Dad took off his jumper and tied it to a small tree that was growing quite close to the opening of the chimney.

"That'll serve as a marker in case someone has to come and find me as well", he muttered under his breath. He looked back down the chimney and saw that the children had scattered the fire and the flames were out. Smoke had stopped billowing from the chimney and he was able to take a good look down. The chimney was probably about a metre wide with fairly, straight sides. He sat down on the edge and swung his feet over the side. "Right stand back out of the way. I'm coming down." He pushed himself off over the side. With his back against one side and his feet, directly out in front of him, pressed firmly against the opposite wall he gradually inched himself down.

The children stood below watching his progress their hearts in their mouths hardly daring to draw breath.

"Oh Daddy do be careful", Josey couldn't help herself. Her concern brought tears to her eyes once again.

"It's OK Jo. I'll be alright", he grunted.

Half way down the chimney, he stopped and looked hard at the opposite wall where his feet were braced.

"Oh! There's a little hole in the wall here and there seems to be something lodged in it. Look out below. I've just got to kick it out. I don't want it to fall on me once I've got past. It seems to be quite loose." Gingerly, he pushed and kicked with one heel at a loose rock in the opposite wall. The children turned to each other and cried out in unison, "Dad it's the treasure!"

Kitty went on to explain, "We saw it earlier but couldn't reach it and then well, we all forgot about it. It's Cap'n Billy Bones' treasure."

The children clutched each other excitedly watching avidly for the 'treasure' to appear. Dad kicked and kicked and eventually he dislodged the rock that tumbled down the chimney bouncing across the cavern floor. After the rock came a very large sack, which hit the cavern floor with a thud spilling part of its contents on impact. Gold coins glistened in the fading sunlight and reflected the candlelight back into their eager, smoke blackened faces.

"It's the treasure Dad", Sam called up watching his father continue to inch his way down the shaft. As he reached the bottom of the chimney, Dad called out, "Move that out of the way I've got to jump."

The children rushed forward and between them dragged the sack back as far as they could. Kitty called, "OK" and Dad pushed off with his hands allowing his feet to fall from the other wall at exactly the same time. He came down feet first hitting the floor with a frightful bump.

Josey rushed forward, "Oh Daddy, Daddy are you OK?" Tears were streaming down her face as she threw her arms around him.

"I'm alright Jo, don't worry", he wrapped Josey in his arms and Kitty and Sam rushed into his embrace. "Group hug", he called as he held them all close, safe in his arms.

"Well it seems to me you've had quite an adventure. You can tell me all about it as we make our way back to the cellar. Mum is quite worried and you've missed dinner you must be starving. Now come on show me the way out of this place. I warn you Mum and I will want a pretty good explanation as to why you skipped off and put yourselves in danger without telling us or anyone else where you were going." He tried to look serious and stern but his joy at finding them all safe and sound simply wouldn't let the smile disappear from his face. He hugged them all again and they all picked themselves up and dusted themselves down. Josey clung on to her Daddy's hand for all she was worth. She thought she might never let go of him again such was her relief at being rescued. Sam immediately went to the treasure sack, which they had dragged out of the way of Dad's fall while Kitty bent to retrieve the candles that had fallen from her pocket. In her pocket, she found her torch and turned it on walking over to join the others who had clustered around Sam and the treasure sack. Dad was examining some of the gold coins in the pale light, which was shining down the chimney.

"Well these seem real enough to me. It seems you really have found treasure. We'd better take it with us. I'm afraid just for a little while Josey you're going to have to let go of my hand. This sack is quite heavy and I shall need both hands to lift it. Now who's going to be the guide? Come on Sam you lead the way. We'll need more light than that torch so keep those candles burning Kitty, you and Josey can hold one each."

Kitty passed a candle to Josey and lit another from the supply in her pocket while Sam retrieved the two cutlasses from the floor and prepared to lead the way back up the tunnel to safety. As they walked out of the cleft back to the cavern proper, they turned and had a last look back up the chimney and Cap'n Billy's window that had saved them. The sunlight flashed and the wind blew a last deep moaning groan as they made their way past the skeletons and back up the tunnel. The children pouring out their tale as they went. Poor Dad had to bend every now and then to negotiate the low ceiling but eventually they came to the back of the cask and Dad marvelled at it as they walked through and into the cellar proper. Sam pushed the front of the giant cask back into place, and it closed with a sharp snick and looking at the casks standing there it was difficult for any of the children to believe that there actually was a tunnel behind it. However, the sound of the gold coins chinking in the treasure sack as they walked was enough to remind them all that it was real. What an adventure!

Dad placed the sack on the floor and with Sam shining the torch over his shoulder up to the trapdoor he climbed the steps, placed his shoulder to the trapdoor and heaved with legs and arms. The trapdoor moved upwards with a sharpness that surprised them all. It crashed against the wall and they heard voices crying, "What's that?" Suddenly into view came the faces of Mum and Mrs Franklyn.

"What on earth are you doing down there?" Mum cried, "and why didn't you tell me you'd found them?" Standing with her hands on her hips, arms akimbo she directed a wrathful look at the children's Daddy. He smiled up at her and descended the steps helping each one of the children up in turn and bringing up the rear himself clutching the treasure sack of gold coins, which bulged in his grip.

"Now before you start to give us all earache", he said, "Let's just go and get a nice cup of tea and have a sit down.

The children have quite a story to tell but I believe that first, they need a drink and something to eat. Is that alright with you Mrs Franklyn? Could you rustle up some sandwiches and tea for us all to have in the bar? The children's story has a lot to do with you as well so I think it would be a good idea if you had tea with us. If you don't mind that is?"

Mrs Franklyn smiled and said, "Well I'm just so pleased that the children are safe. We were all so worried. If there's a story to be told and tea, sandwiches and cakes to be consumed then I think it would be better if you all joined me in my private parlour where we'll be undisturbed. However, might I suggest that the children and you brush yourselves down first, you're all covered in dust and cobwebs", she wrinkled her nose as if they all had a bad smell to go with the dirt. "I'll order the tea now and you can meet me upstairs in five minutes", she bustled away all smiles.

Mum was about to cross question them all and give them a sever ticking off but Dad intervened. "Ok darling I know you're cross and we all know you were very worried but if half the things I've heard from the children are true we'd be better, for the moment to reserve our judgement and listen to their story before we start to think about punishing them. Let's just be glad we got them back safe and sound."

Mum smiled and relented, "You're right", she said and for the first time relaxed and gathered them all into a hug before shepherding them all off to the bathroom for a wash and brush up. She insisted that Sam could not take the two cutlasses and these were passed to Dad who carried the cutlasses and the treasure sack away to Mrs Franklyn's parlour before tidying himself up and joining them all. When he arrived, the children were busily showing the gold coins, the candles, the treasure map and the rhyme to a shell shocked Mum and Mrs Franklyn.

"Well I'm blessed. Well I'm blessed." Mrs Franklyn repeated over and over again, staring from one to the other. "Well I'm blessed. Who'd have thought it?"

Mum sat there stopping the story every now and then to ask a question, issue a reprimand and then direct the children back to the story at the relevant point. While the children vied with each other to boost their own part of the adventure and prove to all concerned how brave and strong and courageous they were. As Dad walked into the room Josey left the group and hurried over to hold his hand. She had not really recovered quite yet and only her Daddy's reassuring presence was going to settle her mind.

While Kitty continued with the story Sam, having got bored with Mum's constant interruptions, started to take the heavy gold coins from the bag and pile them up in stacks of ten. Josey pulled her Dad over to the table and they both started to help Sam. Eventually they all started to pile up the coins while Kitty, somewhat filled with her own self-importance, continued to hold forth on the great adventure, telling and retelling her part in the story.

When the story finally ended in the triumphant exit from the cellar and the final coin had been stacked, they all looked down to see the coffee table literally covered in stacks of coins. Hundreds of them, glistening and glinting in the light cast by the small chandelier that hung in the centre of the room.

"Well", said Sam, "I know what I'm going to spend my share on."

This made everyone laugh, as Sam went on to describe computer games and off-road four-wheel drive quad bikes.

Dad interrupted him, "You're not going to be spending any of this money I'm afraid Sam." Then at the distraught look on Sam's face, "Well not yet anyway."

"What do you mean? We found it it's ours surely?" Sam looked astonished.

"I'm afraid this is what's called 'Treasure Trove' and it has to be reported to the authorities. We'll have to hand it over to the Police or the local Coroner. I forget which, they will then decide if we can keep it or if it belongs to The Crown."

"What's The Crown?" Sam asked belligerently. "We found it what's it got to do with anyone else?"

Kitty and Josey nodded their heads in agreement saying, "Oh that's not fair."

Dad shushed them and said, "Look I'm very sorry but it's the law. Cap'n Bones probably stole the treasure and we are not going to continue down that criminal path. If we just kept it that would be wrong and I'm afraid I'm not prepared to let you become criminal masterminds at such an early age. When you get older you'll probably do that for yourselves, you're such an unruly lot", he teased ruffling Sam's hair and giving both the girls a squeeze.

"No seriously we have no choice in the matter. We must report it but that doesn't mean you won't get something from it. The Coroner may well decide it's not Treasure Trove in which case all of this will belong to you." He indicated the massive pile of gold on the table but if it is classified as Treasure Trove I think you'll simply get a reward but whatever happens you will get something and you've had an adventure that will last you a lifetime."

The children looked at each other grinning from ear to ear, Sam's computer games were suddenly back on the menu.

"Now Mrs Franklyn", Dad continued, "You must have a say in this. You are the legal owner of the map and probably the tunnel and therefore the treasure itself. What do you want to do with it?"

The children turned to Mrs Franklyn they hadn't thought that the treasure might belong to her at all. Mrs Franklyn saw the disappointment mirrored in their upturned faces and smiled benignly. "Don't you worry my dears. I wouldn't think of claiming any part of this treasure it belongs to you. After all, you did all the hard work, following the map and making sense of the rhyme. I would never have been clever enough or brave enough to do that. No, I'm very content living here in my lovely little hotel and when the story breaks in the papers, I shall probably find myself inundated with people wanting to see the tunnel and hear the story. All I shall want from you is a promise to come back and see me from time to time. I'm so glad that you came and I shall be so glad to see you all again next year and perhaps the year after. The holiday wasn't so bad after all was it my dears?"

They all agreed that they had never spent a better holiday and Dad said, "That's very kind of you Mrs Franklyn of course we shall come back. We would have done anyway even if the children hadn't found the treasure. This 'Holiday in The Rain' has turned out quite well hasn't it?" he added.

"You see as I've always said 'Treasure is Where You Find It' and for us, being together is the very best treasure there could ever be."

THE END

Printed in Great Britain
by Amazon

65799505R00092